Letters to Tim

Louis Elliott

PAGE PUBLISHING, INC.
New York, NY

First originally published by Page Publishing, Inc. 2017

ISBN 978-1-68409-290-1 (Paperback)
ISBN 978-1-68409-291-8 (Digital)

Printed in the United States of America

To Tim, who without his encouragement to keep on writing, this book would perhaps never have been finished. Thanks, Tim, for all your interest and appreciation of my letters.

"A poignant story about a large family going through the challenges of struggles during the depression era, the war years, etc.—"

November 13, 2014

Dear Tim,

    I hope you're having a good week and will continue to get better day by day! In the classic movie *Bambi* by Walt Disney, there's a scene I like and think of when I'm somewhat down on life. It's a beautiful early spring morning in the forest. The sun is shining brightly, the birds are singing, and the forest is coming alive with sounds. The little fawn, Bambi, bounds up to his mother, his eyes sparkle and are full of eagerness, and in an excited voice, he says, "Well, mother, what are we going to do today?" He could hardly contain his excitement as to what new adventures awaited him that day! Sometimes as I sit in the forest hunting and observing the dawn appearing, I'm reminded of the wonderful opportunities we have to say, "What am I going to do today?"

    I'd like to write to you today about your great-grandfather. Of course, you never had the opportunity of meeting him. He was born in 1895 and lived until 1979 when he died in a car crash. He was a small man of stature, probably only about five feet and five inches tall. He never weighed over 130 pounds his entire life. He was often referred to as a "wiry" little man—this meaning he was full of energy, always on the go, and focused on getting things done. At age seventy-five, he cut down pine trees then dragged them up the steep hillside with a mule and constructed a new corn crib approximately twenty-five by twenty-five square feet including a loft! His name was John Joseph Elliott II, but everyone simply called him Jonny. I suppose this was to avoid the confusion between Jonny and his father, John Joseph Elliott I. Jonny was the second oldest of seven children. His older sister, Fanny, was the first born, then Jonny, Mary, Nell, William, George, and Ethyl. They were reared in the beautiful but rugged foothills of the Appalachian mountain range in the coal mining region of north central Alabama. His father, John Joseph I, was in poor health and he died when he was only about fifty years old. Jonny was pressed into being the bread winner early in life. He only finished the sixth grade before leaving school and going to work in the coal mine to earn money for the family. He was twelve years old! Back then, a child of twelve years old could be legally hired to do a man's job. Forty years of work in the coal mine took its toll on Jonny. He suffered two accidents in the mine, which left him with chronic back pain. His hands, knees, and feet were crippled with arthritis, and he was later diagnosed with black lung disease due to the coal dust he breathed all those years.

After working approximately five years in the coal mine, Jonny was drafted into the military. At approximately nineteen years old, Jonny was sent to Europe to fight in the First World War. He served mostly as a cook and was very proud of his military service for his country. Later, after World War II, Jonny joined the local American Legion and Veterans of Foreign Wars organizations. He attended their monthly meetings faithfully, and it became a town tradition on Armistice Day for Jonny to cook his own recipe of army stew and feed the entire town! Most of the surviving pictures of Jonny are pictures of him in his army uniform or VFW hat. He talked very little about his time spent in the military. He spoke of being in Europe and perhaps he experienced the horrors of trench warfare and poison gas, but he never once talked about it. He had a very strange way of walking. Both feet would splay outward as he walked. He stated that's the way he was trained to walk and march when he was in the army. The rational was that if you flared your toes outward as you walked, you were less likely to trip over your own feet and fall. As a child, I could easily identify Dad's footprints in the dust along the road due to this unique way of walking.

World War I was fought in Europe between 1914 and 1918. The allies of England, France, and Russia fought primarily against Germany, Austria, Italy, and later, Turkey. The United States initially chose to stay out of this conflict; however, when a German submarine sank the *Lusitania*, an English cruise ship in 1915, killing 128 Americans on board, the attitude of the United States slowly changed, and the United States entered the war in 1917. Estimates are that between eight and nine million soldiers died in this war. Russia suffered the most deaths with a loss of one and three quarter million soldiers. A truce was reached on November 11, 1918, and the war ended. The Treaty of Versailles was signed by the allies in 1919. President Woodrow Wilson very much opposed the terms in this agreement as it placed sole responsibility for the war on Germany. Germany lost a great deal of territory, had major military restraints placed on her, and was assessed a very large reparation. With the ensuing Great Depression during the 1930s, the German government collapsed into anarchy, which was a major factor contributing to the rise of Hitler into power during the midthirties.

Sometime around 1918 or 1919, Jonny returned home from the war. I believe it was before being discharged from the army that Jonny met his future bride, Vora Johnson. Jonny never talked about how he won the heart of Vora. Maybe it was the handsome man in the army uniform. At age sixteen, Vora became Jonny's bride. Jonny purchased forty acres of property from his uncle and built a home for his young bride. Most of the work was done on the home by Jonny and his younger brother, George. It wasn't a fancy home by today's standards. It just provided basic shelter from the elements. It had six rooms: three bedrooms on the south side and a sitting room, dining room, and kitchen on the north side. There was no indoor plumbing, no running water, and initially, no electricity and no central heating. Once electricity was acquired, it was used almost exclusively for evening lighting. The single lightbulb hanging from a suspended electrical wire in the middle of the room replaced the old kerosene lamps previously used. For heat, there was a small stone chimney that had back to back fireplaces. One served the main bedroom and the opposite one served the sitting room. The sitting room fireplace was seldom used. None of the bedrooms had heat. Sometime after the house was built, a back porch was added that enclosed the well which provided the water. All the water used was taken from this well by hand, cranking a bucket attached to a rope which raised or lowered the bucket. A two-gallon bucket usually sat on a small table near the well. A dipper was in this bucket and universally used by anyone who wished a drink of water. After getting their drink, the dipper was returned into the bucket of water. Unsanitary? Sometimes dead bees or moths had to be skimmed off before getting your drink! Sometimes when visitors came, a fresh bucket of cool water was drawn from the well just for them.

After returning from the war, getting married, and building a house, Jonny returned to working in the coal mines. People said he outworked men twice his size and no one loaded more coal per day than Jonny. He was a quiet man but a man who was keenly aware of world affairs. He read his newspaper faithfully every day. Most often in the evening, after supper and the evening chores were done, Jonny would get his pipe, pack it with Prince Albert smoking tobacco, and spend the rest of the evening until bed time reading his newspaper from cover to cover. Later when electricity was in the house, Jonny would listen intently to the evening news on the radio. When the kids were sharing this room in the evening, they knew not to make a sound while the news was on the radio.

Within ten years after Jonny and Vora were married, they had four children (more were to come). John Joseph III was the first, then James Howard, Frances, and Vera Nell. After all these children were born, Jonny began farming to help feed and clothe his family. During the spring, summer, and fall, there was planting, cultivating, and harvesting of crops such as cotton, corn, and potatoes, When Jonny got home from the coal mines, he would hitch up his team of mules and plow until dark. As John Jr., and James got older, they assumed much of the farming chores every day when they got home from school. By age twelve, both John Jr. and James had learned how to hitch up a team of horses and plow and cultivate the crops. With the addition of these two new workers, Jonny leased additional land from his uncle down along the river. This land was referred to as the bottom land.

Over the next five years, three additional children were born. These were Fred, and then a big surprise, twins named Lois and Louis.

Jonny's days and years remained very much the same: work, work, work, His evenings remained very much the same. Although poorly educated, Jonny learned to be proficient in his reading skills. The mailman would deliver the newspaper every day, and Jonny remained well informed on local and national news. He avidly studied upcoming state and national elections and never failed to exercise his right to vote. Being a coal miner, he recognized John L. Lewis as one of his greatest heroes. John L. Lewis was responsible for unionizing coal miners nationally and greatly improved miner's wages and mine safety. Jonny idolized this man with the huge bushy eyebrows!

Modernization came slowly to this remote region of Alabama. Horses and wagons would fill the back alleys behind the stores in the small mining towns every Saturday. The rural folks came to town to purchase their weekly supply of staples and dry goods. It was still more common to see horse-drawn wagons rather than cars on the main street until well into the 1940s. Coal burning steam engines were common along the railroad side tracks as they brought the coal cars full of coal to the main trunk line to be moved north.

Life for Jonny and his family changed very little until the beginning of World War Two. He worked in the coal mine eight to ten hours per day, came home and farmed until dark, then finally he would take a bath in a galvanized wash tub in the front room by the fireplace. This was the only room in the house with solid wooden doors. All the other bedrooms simply had curtains separating them from the other rooms. The bath water was heated in the water jacket on the kitchen cook stove.

His day would begin about 6:00 a.m. Jonny always got up first. During the winter, it was a welcome sound to the children to hear Jonny clanging a poker in the fireplace in the front room. It meant they would have a warm place to dress for school in another thirty minutes. Just before going to bed at night, Jonny would cover the coals in the fireplace with ashes from underneath the grate which almost extinguished the fire. It would smolder all night, and the next morning the clanging of the poker meant the fire was being brought back to life. Once the fire was started in the front bedroom, Jonny would go to the kitchen and start a fire in the cook stove. By then Vora was up and would come to the kitchen to start breakfast for her family. She began by making biscuits from the flour stored in the five-gallon metal pail in the pantry. Jonny would light a lantern, grab the two-gallon milk bucket and his coat, and head out to the barn to milk the cow. This would take twenty to thirty minutes, depending on the mood of the cow! When this task was done, Jonny would come back into the house, stopping briefly by the stove to warm his cold hands. Vora now had his breakfast of hot biscuits, eggs, some white side meat, and hot coffee ready. (White side meat is the same as bacon except the white meat was not smoked or seasoned in any way like bacon.) After finishing his breakfast, Jonny would grab his metal lunch bucket and a gallon jug of water, then head out the door while it was still dark to walk three miles to catch his ride to the mine. The coal company had a truck they sent to pick up the miners in a designated spot. Usually twelve to fifteen miners rode in the back of this truck, rain or shine, summer and winter to get to their jobs.

This hard life never seemed to be a source of discouragement for Jonny. He took everything in stride. If I were to try to define contentment, I would say it was Jonny in the evening. After evening chores, his supper, and bath, Jonny would take a seat in his rocking chair by the fireplace, read his paper from cover to cover, and then listen to the evening news on the radio. Jonny would finish his newspaper then pull his rocker up close to the warm fire, pull the red can of Prince Albert smoking tobacco from his pocket, pack the tobacco in his pipe, light it with a match, and sit there until bedtime. He just gazed into the flickering flames from the fire, occasionally spitting into the fire which made a hissing sound that amused the children. Seldom saying a word, tired, relaxed, comfortable, Jonny seemed to be assessing the day's activities and concluding, "All is well, I'll rest tonight and sleep well, and when morning comes, I'll be ready to face the new day! Life is hard but good."

Jonny was:

- A generous man. Relatives and friends who came for a visit from the city never left without a large bag filled with fresh vegetables from the garden, sweet potatoes, or fresh fruit in season.
- A confident man. What man do you know who would go into town wearing his wife's high-heeled shoes? Vora's new mail-ordered shoes were too tight, so Jonny wore them all day to stretch them for her, even wearing them into town!
- A considerate man. He convinced his children that his favorite part of the chicken was the neck and back bone in order for the children to get the breast, legs, and thighs.
- A stern man. There were only rare times when he laughed. He was firm with the kids. Never did the kids ever hear expressions like, "Do you want me to kiss your boo boo?" If the boys ever came in with a sprained ankle or sore knee from rough housing with each other, Jonny would say, "That's what you get for that kind of foolishness!" No sympathy! No outward expressions of love or affection. That was the role of the mother not the man of the house.

- An honest man. Jonny carried a line of credit at the local grocery store. Every payday, he would stop by the store to pay his bill. Then he would buy a whole stick of bologna, tuck it under his arm, and walk home. (A stick of bologna was about four inches in diameter and about sixteen inches long.)

Jonny stated, "I'll never get on an airplane unless I can have one foot dragging!" (At about age seventy-five, he did ride a plane from Detroit to Birmingham, Alabama.)

If the older children came home for a visit and continued to visit and talk past Jonny's bedtime, he would get up from his chair and announce, "Well, the wind's not blowing and nobody's sick, so I'm going to bed!"

If he heard something someone planned to do that he thought to be foolish, he would exclaim, "That's the most bone levelish thing I've ever heard."(I don't know where this expression originated from, but I suspect it was solely from Jonny.)

Jonny never cursed, never drank, never gambled, and never gossiped—but he certainly did love his Prince Albert smoking tobacco. The hillside behind the barn was littered with those bright red empty tobacco tins!

Sequel

By today's standards, Jonny might have been considered a child abuser. He always had a wide leather strap, probably a piece salvaged from a worn-out horse harness, hanging on the wall behind the kitchen stove. It was seldom used but hung there as a reminder to the children that misbehavior would not be tolerated. When it was used, it made a lasting impression! Jonny was stern with the boys, and they felt the girls got off to easy. I don't ever remember him using the strap on the girls.

The children didn't fear Jonny but rather held a deep respect for him as their provider. This dictated how they should behave around him. When he came home from the coal mine each day, the children would carefully assess the mood he was in. If he was grouchy, they knew to keep their distance. At the evening meal, Jonny would outline what the boy's jobs would be the next day (the girls duties were given by their mother). Plowing the corn fields, weeding the garden, gathering over-ripe vegetables and wind-fall fruit for the pigs, or mending the pasture fence, to name just a few duties frequently assigned. The list seemed endless!

The children learned to be independent, resourceful, and tough at an early age. If they received a nasty cut or splinter, they took care of it themselves. They amused themselves by making most of their own toys. Wooden guns were cut and shaped from a sapling carefully selected to resemble a gun stock and barrel. Small scraps of wood were nailed together to resemble a toy truck or wagon. Elaborate miniature roads were smoothed out in the dust underneath the front porch to play with the homemade toy trucks. The older children would fashion swings using wild grape vines found hanging from a sturdy tree along a hillside. They would swing Tarzan style from these vines. Occasionally the vines would break, resulting in a nasty fall. Sometimes attempts to ride a neighbor's steer in the pasture would result in bumps and bruises. Most injuries remained unreported to the parents unless they were too obvious to be concealed.

Tom Brokaw dubbed this generations of Americans as "America's greatest generation." This was the generation of young men who responded to the defense of our nation in World War II. Their courage, unselfish sacrifices, and guts won the war and preserved our freedom.

The stern, strong discipline of Jonny Elliott was not a unique trait. Rather, it was a social trait indigenous to all rural fathers of that era. As I recall, all my friends had fathers with very similar traits. Most, I would say, were even sterner than Jonny. In some cases, this sternness went over the limit. Some children frequently showed evidence of abuse, most often when their fathers were drinking. The children would show signs of severe abuse. Then the line would be crossed from sternness to abuse. I was always amazed at the resilience of these children. They just seemed strong enough to deal with whatever came their way!

The question begging for an answer is: is there a mutual ground somewhere between the stern, heavy-handed discipline of fathers three or four generations ago and the permissive, coddling era of today? Recently in a large retail store, I observed a young family leaving with their grocery cart full and a small child walking slightly behind them (a girl about four years old). As they passed the arcade with the flashing lights and amusing sounds, the young girl made an abrupt left turn into the arcade. The father called for the young girl, "Come on, we've got to go!" No response from the child. He again called out, "Come on, we've got to go see grandma!" No response. A third time. "Come on, Lisa, I don't have any money." No response! Finally, the father went back, picked up the child in his arms and took her screaming and kicking out of the store. I don't claim to be a trained psychologist or an expert in child behavior, but have we come too far in our permissive society?

I don't recall a single incident in all my school years where a child brought a gun to school. There was ample opportunities. Almost every home had a shotgun or rifle above the fireplace or hanging on the bedroom wall. Yet never do I recall a single incident where a child came to school with a weapon and created an act of terrorism among his classmates. Are children today permitted too much freedom and have no fear of consequences for poor choices? Is there no authoritative figure in their lives, one they recognize as the one to whom they must justify their deeds and actions and must face the consequences if they provoke his wrath?

Seems to me that the leather strap hanging on the wall behind the stove has been removed, but what has taken its place?

Much love.

Hi Tim,

We hope week by week you're feeling better, and I hope my letters will provide some interesting reading for you. In this letter, I'd like to introduce you to your great-grandmother.

Her maiden name was Vora Johnson (born in February 1903). She was the oldest of four daughters born to James and Rose Johnson. The grandchildren called them Ma Rosy and Pa Jim. The Johnsons enjoyed a degree of social status in the small town of approximately 2,500 people. James, or Jim as most people called him, was employed by the United States Postal Service. He delivered mail on a designated rural route in Walker County, Alabama. While not viewed as a member of the upper class, comprised of merchants, bankers, doctors, and coal mine owners, Jim and Rose were considered model citizens of this small town. Their house was on a city lot approximately 100 feet wide but extended back about 250 feet. The house was constructed of milled wood siding, neatly painted white with a red brick foundation.

The home had an L-shaped porch, which spanned all across the front of the house as well as continuing around the east side. Much time was spent by Rose and her group of lady friends on this front porch. From the porch, there were two entrance ways into the house. One door opened into what was referred to as the sitting parlor, and the other door opened into the front bedroom. There was an upright piano in the parlor. I'm not certain as to how many of the girls played the piano, but Vora was very musical talented and she played the piano very well. The family spent most of the time in the evening in the front bedroom by the open fireplace. On the east side of the house was the bedrooms, and on the west side was the parlor, a dining room, and the kitchen. There was a small enclosed structure extending out from the kitchen, which contained a hand-operated water pump which was used to pump water up out of a cistern. The cistern was just outside the kitchen in the backyard. It was made of concrete. It was dug out into the ground about four feet deep, and it extended above the ground approximately five feet. It was about ten feet wide and perhaps fifteen feet long. The entire top was enclosed with a concrete cover. I think all the water used by the family came from this cistern. Gutters on the house directed the rain water from the roof into pipes which emptied into the cistern. In 1937, city water became available and replaced this cistern; however, the cistern remained in place and still held water. A small portion of the backyard was enclosed with a six foot wire fence. The backyard extended perhaps twenty-five feet from the back of the house to the fence. Beyond this fenced in yard was the corral for the horses.

Jim's mail route was long enough and the quantity of mail large enough that he needed a two-horse buggy to accommodate the load of mail. The buggy was enclosed with sides and a top to protect the mail from the weather. Beyond the corral, there was a gate leading out to a back alley. An outhouse was located just inside the alley, which required a trek through the horse corral to do your business. Once a week, a honey wagon would come through the back alley to collect and replace the pots beneath the seat in the outhouse. As an adult, Vora often laughed about the time she was sitting on the toilet and the sanitation engineer pulled the collection pot out from under her seat!

Vora was very frightened of thunderstorms. At age twelve, a tornado ripped the roof off their house! Vora described how she heard this loud roar and not knowing what it was, she went to the front door to investigate. Just as she opened the door, the tornado struck the house, ripping the roof off, and left her standing in the door frame. From that traumatic experience forward, Vora had a great fear of storms, even if they didn't appear very severe.

Vora met Jonny when she was sixteen and in the eleventh grade. She was very intelligent and most likely an excellent student. Neither Vora nor Jonny ever discussed how or why they made the decision to get married and for Vora to leave school. Many times, however, Vora expressed regrets for failing to finish high school. Maybe it was because all three of her younger sisters completed high school and two of them went on to college and became teachers. Even though Vora never finished high school, she was very capable of helping the children with their homework. She was an excellent speller, good in math, and wrote many interesting letters to relatives and friends. Letter writing was a very important means of communication. There were no telephones. Vora would often write three or four letters per week.

Considering their diverse childhood backgrounds, one could wonder how this marriage was formed and how it survived; but survive it did! After being married approximately two years, Vora became pregnant with her first born, John Jr. For the next fifteen years, there was a new baby about every two and half to three years. By the time Vora had reached thirty-two years of age, she had given birth to seven children!

Vora never worked outside the home her entire life. However, what she accomplished in her role of wife and mother ranks second to none in job performance. When you consider the challenges confronting her in raising her large family of seven children, without any of our modern conveniences, it's amazing when compared with the modern housewife with all her conveniences. "Man works from sun to sun, but woman's work is never done."

Early in the morning, Vora would arise from the bed, even if she had been interrupted from sleep to caring for a sick child. She would begin her day by preparing breakfast for Jonny and the children. Her cooking skills were quite good, considering the limited control she had of maintaining a constant temperature in the wood and coal burning stove. A damper on the stove pipe vent was her only way of crudely regulating the oven temperature. Biscuits and cakes had to be constantly monitored to prevent them from burning. Except for the summer months when the children were out of school, Vora had to prepare not only breakfast but pack lunches for all the children and Jonny. In the summertime, preparing for the noon meal began almost immediately after breakfast was finished! This required gathering the vegetables from the garden, cleaning and preparing them, then cooking them. For meat, frequently she had to kill a chicken or make a trip out to the smoke house to slice off some pork buried in the salt in the meat box. Vora would often milk the cow in the evening, relieving Jonny of that task if it appeared he wasn't going to make it home before dark. Most of the milk from the morning and evening milking was consumed by the children that day. Any leftover was poured into a churn by the cook stove to ripen in order to make butter. Vora referred to this process as clabbering the milk.

Vora changed and washed many diapers while raising her brood of seven. Washing diapers and the children's clothing was a major undertaking. Usually the washing was done in a large cast iron kettle located outside in the backyard. First, about fifteen gallons of water had to be drawn from the well then transferred to the kettle out in the yard. A fire was built under the kettle to get the water hot. Once the water was hot, some lye soap was added and then the clothes. Diapers, the children's clothes, and Jonny's coal dust filled work clothes all had to be washed separately. Once the clothes were boiling in the hot water, a large wooden paddle was used to agitate or stir the clothes. Most of the children's clothes would require taking the clothes from the kettle, scrubbing them using a hand wash board, then putting them back into the kettle for a final boiling. From the final boiling, the clothes were transferred to a large wash tub of clear fresh water. They were agitated again in order to rinse all the soap from the clothes. Then they were transferred to a dry tub to be taken to the clothes line to be hung up to dry. Of course as the children got older, they helped with the clothes washing as well. On one occasion, when Vora was washing Jonny's work clothes, she decided one pair was too torn and tattered to wash and decided she would just burn them. She tossed them into the fire beneath the kettle. Suddenly there were several loud explosions which came from the fire! It seems Jonny had inadvertently left some blasting caps (a blasting cap was a small igniter inserted into the much more powerful black powder explosives which caused it to explode) in the pockets of his work clothes. Vora was alleged to have yelled, "Run in the house, kids, your pa's pants are exploding!"

With all the work needing to be done and with all those children underfoot, Vora sometimes would get upset and lose her temper (mostly with the boys). When this happened, she would eject all the kids from the house then calmed down, taking advantage of a little peace and quiet. Once calmed down, Vora would go outside and tell the children, "If you're ready to behave, then you can come back inside the house." Vora's temperament was quite different from Jonny's. When frustrated, she would sometimes have a meltdown and cry. Once she had a good cry, she would quickly return to normal and continue with her normal chores. During World War II, with the two older boys in the military, Vora would listen very intently to the radio every time the war news would come on. She would often fall to her knees and pray if the war news was bad.

Vora never used the leather strap hanging behind the kitchen stove. If provoked long enough, she would resort to an open palm swatting, and if upset enough, anywhere on a child's body was fair game! Most of the time, she used a switch. A lilac bush grew just outside the kitchen door. It had long straight canes about three-eighth inch in diameter at the base and tapered to a thin flexible end about two feet long. Vora used this often to sting the bare legs of an unruly child. One of the children, I won't reveal which one, tried several times to kill that ole lilac bush by pouring hot water on it!

One Sunday morning, as all the children were scurrying around getting ready to go to church, the younger boys, Fred and Louis, got into a skirmish in the kitchen. Fred was about fifteen and Louis was eleven. Vora had a churn full of milk sitting on a kitchen chair near the stove. Fred gave Louis a big shove and Louis fell backwards into that churn. The churn fell off the chair and landed upside down on the kitchen floor. The thick buttermilk began gurgling out from under the churn mouth and slowly spreading across the kitchen floor. Everyone froze for a few seconds, not knowing just what to do. Vora began yelling at the boys! "You kids are going to drive me absolutely crazy!" The churn continued to make a *glug, glug, glug* sound as the buttermilk slowly crept across the kitchen floor. Louis quickly tried to upright the churn. In the process, as the churn was lifted off the floor, an additional two or three gallons of buttermilk spilled onto the floor. Louis ran into the front room and grabbed the ash shovel and ash bucket from near the fireplace. He quickly began scooping the oozing buttermilk into the ash bucket. Vora continued to yell. Soon the buttermilk was corralled, and Fred brought the mop in with a bucket of water to rinse the floor. The floor was mopped somewhat clean. We all loaded into Dad's old truck and went to church. Louis wondered what his fate would be when we got back home from church. Would there be a good whipping awaiting from Dad? He was angry with Fred for pushing him back into the churn and causing the accident. He didn't feel he disserved to be punished because it was all Fred's fault. During the church service, people sitting near us began turning their heads around and sniffing the air. Why did they smell buttermilk in the church building? We forgot to clean our shoes!

Fred and Louis sat quietly in church. Their thoughts were on what was going to happen when they got back home. The preacher preached about love, mercy, and forgiveness. Vora seemed to listen intently. As we arrived back home from church, we entered the back door into the kitchen. The strong odor of buttermilk reminded us of what had happened. Vora seemed calmed by the preacher's words. She looked at the churn and began to chuckle. She broke out into laughter and stated, "That was a pretty funny sight, all that buttermilk oozing out from under that churn!" Everyone laughed, but Dad said, "I've told you boys to keep your horseplay outside. If anything like this ever happens again, you're going to be in for a good whipping." Fred and Louis were very thankful for that preacher's sermon. No doubt, it saved them from a good whipping! Louis was still very angry with Fred. How could he get even with Fred?

It was about three weeks before Christmas. A local radio station had just begun to read letters to Santa over the air each morning from local children. The station encouraged the children to send Santa their wish list as to what they wanted Santa to bring them. Louis secretly wrote a letter to Santa and mailed it to the radio station. It read, "Dear Santa, I would like a teddy bear, lots of fruit, nuts, and candy, and two packages of double-edged razor blades! Signed, Little Freddy Elliott!" Louis hoped Santa would read the letter over the air. Louis told some of Fred's friends to listen to the station for the next several days. Sure enough, the radio Santa read the letter over the air and gave a big ho, ho, ho after he read it! The Files boys and Sonny Childers heard this, and Fred was teased unmercifully way beyond Christmas. Fred said, "If I ever find out who sent that letter, I'm going to kick their tail all over this mountain!" Louis felt vindicated. Getting even is not always such a bad thing!

Amazingly, Vora somehow found time to sew dresses for the girls and shirts for the boys! She also found time to make numerous quilts for the beds. Nothing fancy, just very warm and functional. Since there was no heat in the bedrooms, each bed required three or four quilts in the wintertime to keep the children warm. Often when the children would first awaken in the morning, they could see their breath in the cold morning air!

In the late spring and summer months, additional chores of canning, drying, and preserving food for winter's use was added to an already heavy load. Many quart jars of green beans, tomatoes, and corn were canned. Canning required a hot fire in the kitchen stove. Oftentimes the normal outside temperature would be 85 to 100 degrees. Inside the kitchen, it would soar to 110 to 115 degrees. Vora also made many jars of jelly from wild blackberries, peaches, plums, and apples. One of the very special treats for the children was her fig preserves. A fig tree grew on the south side of the house, somewhat protected from the winter cold by the southern exposure to the sun. Though considered a semi-tropical tree, this fig tree usually survived the winter unless it was an extremely harsh year. In such cases, the fig tree would be killed back to the roots, but within two years, it would be back in full production. Most years it would produce more fruit than Vora could use, and the surplus crop was sold to waiting customers. There were always more people seeking to buy the figs than Vora could supply.

During the depression years, Vora's management skills proved to be a vital asset for the financial survival of the family. Though cash money was very scarce, she managed to keep the family supplied with sufficient money to buy new winter coats, shoes, and clothing for school. These were usually ordered from a mail-order catalogue. Money was acquired by selling surplus eggs, chickens, butter, and fresh vegetables. Even during the depression, eggs were in high demand and brought about sixty cents per dozen. The children were allowed only one egg at breakfast so the surplus could be sold or exchanged at the grocery store for flour, corn meal, sugar, and coffee. Vegetables which were in good demand most of the time were green beans, okra, cabbage, and new potatoes. Apples and peaches were also sold by the bushel when they were in season. Sometimes, even though the merchant already had an ample supply of fresh vegetables on hand, he would take them anyway when brought to his store. He'd simply put them on special today and help every one of his town customers as well as the rural folks from whom he purchased the vegetables. Everyone helped each other as best they could during the depression years. Jonny kept a brood sow hog on the farm to produce one or two litters of piglets each year. He would normally keep only two or three pigs to raise for his family's use. The others he sold to the neighbors. The sow would usually have a litter of six to eight piglets. A six- or eight-week-old piglet sold for about five dollars. Sometimes neighbors would bargain with Jonny and get the price down to three dollars. Jonny would say, "I never want to take advantage of anybody."

Vora was very resourceful. She found numerous ways to fix the meals each day even though the basic ingredients were the same. Sometimes she would cook black eyed peas, then mash them up, then add some eggs and milk and fry them. Everyone thought they were eating pork sausage! Rarely did a day go by that Vora didn't prepare greens from the garden. Turnip greens, mustard greens, and collard greens could be grown nine months out of the year. They were simply pinched off the stalk daily and fresh leaves would then grow back. Pork grease or a chunk of fat pork back would be cooked with the greens to add flavor. Jonny always ate the fat. Green beans were often cooked in the same pot with new potatoes. Vora would dig under the potato vines and search for the small half-grown potatoes. Often they were no larger than marbles. They had a totally different flavor than the fully mature potatoes. The children loved them! Sweet potatoes were baked almost daily and were used as dessert. The potatoes were sliced in half and a generous amount of butter was spread on them. It was good, but sometimes the children grew tired of them every day, and then Vora would make a sweet potato pie which the children would devour. Another favorite dessert was a leftover biscuit from breakfast which was warmed in the oven then split in half. Butter was spread on both halves then sprinkled with sugar and cinnamon. Due to the cost of sugar and cinnamon, this was reserved for special days or Sundays.

Vora was a very healthy woman. She would say, "With this many kids, I can't afford to get sick." I never ever recall her staying in bed due to sickness. Only the birth of a child would confine her for a few days. I'm sure she had colds or flu sometimes, but somehow she managed to pull herself out of bed and managed to get her daily chores done. Fairly often, she would walk about two miles into town to visit her mother. This generally meant carrying an infant in her arms and keeping in tow two or three other young kids walking with her. On Sundays she would get the children ready and walk several miles so they could attend Sunday school.

Vora was neighborly and had a sense of humor. She liked to visit with other neighborhood wives. Sometimes when neighbors would be walking to town, they would often follow the pathway which went right through Vora's yard. They would stop and talk awhile, then the conversation would continue as the neighbor started down the trail toward town. It would continue until the two ladies were literally having to yell at each other in order to hear! Vora enjoyed visits from relatives. Her younger sisters would visit about every month. Vora and her younger sisters would sit on the front porch and laugh and giggle like teenagers! Visiting was the way information was shared. Information about the welfare of other relatives and friends was communicated primarily by relatives' visits or by letters. It served as an information highway and acted as the primary hotline for local news and, unfortunately, for gossip as well.

Perhaps if Vora could have had a crystal ball to peer into when she was sixteen years old and looked at what was in store for her in the future, she might have chosen another pathway. But perhaps not. A mother's love and commitment to her husband and children should never be underestimated. Back then, commitment ranked very high and crossed over social boundaries, no matter what your social status.

Sequel

We often hear people fantasize about the good ole days. They romanticize about life in a by-gone era as being somewhat better and more desirable than our present time. There's even a quarterly magazine published entitled *The Good Ole Days!* Were the days of Vora's era that good? What modern housewife today would trade places with Vora? How many would be willing to give up all their modern conveniences: automatically heated and air conditioned homes, running cold and hot water, modern stoves, refrigerators, microwaves, etc.? Most likely a modern-day housewife would perhaps last less than a week without demanding her modern conveniences back! Today these modern conveniences are considered essential. Back in Vora's days, these would have been considered a luxury!

There are four basic ingredients necessary to sustain life: air to breath, water to drink, food to eat, and shelter from the elements. Anything other than these four elements in past generations would be considered a luxury or fluff as I like to call it. Fluff defines social status. The bigger the home, the most luxurious automobile, the accumulation of wealth are all fluff and not essentials to sustain life. In modern society, fluff has been added as the fifth essential ingredient necessary for survival. Air, water, food, shelter, and fluff.

Many modern-day families expend much of their time and energy accumulating more and more fluff. Sometimes this may cause them to fall into hard times when they don't have financial resources sufficient to provide for all the fluff as well as their essentials.

With the huge expansion of industry at the beginning of the twentieth century, many young adults migrated from the family farm to the jobs in the cities. Young people were attracted to the well-paying urban jobs and to the opportunity to acquire more fluff. They abandoned the family farms. Sadly, today we see thousands of these rural homes that have been abandoned and falling into ruins. These homes thrived during the 1920s, '30s, and '40s. Large barns, which were usually more costly to build than the family's dwelling, are now being allowed to collapse into rotting rubble. These were the farms which thrived and providing the essentials, primarily food, to our growing nation. The desire for more fluff has turned the family run farm into a dinosaur from the past.

During the Great Depression, families living on the family farm were not nearly as devastated as their city cousins. The two essentials that made life so vulnerable in the cities, food and shelter, were generally in ample supply on the family farm. Oftentimes during the depression, family farms were raided by homeless folks seeking food.

Prior to the invention of the farm tractor in the early 1920s, farms were rarely larger than two to three hundred acres. This was all a family could farm, utilizing three or four horses. Now we have tractors (behemoths) capable of farming five thousand acres of farmland. (This displaces upward of three hundred farm families.) Amazing new technology, utilizing global positioning systems, is now being used to guide these tractors without the necessity of a driver!

What will happen if future generations don't need so much fluff? What will happen if they determine it's not essential? Already we're seeing younger generations turning their backs on home ownership. Why invest in a home when it can lose its value overnight? Why should I buy a home when I might move dozens of times during my lifetime? Why should I buy a car when I don't need it? Who needs a car if you live in a high rise in downtown Chicago where you can walk to work or take the subway and have shopping and restaurants within walking distance? But can you grow food in downtown Chicago?

Would our nation be more stable and be less vulnerable to attacks on our food supply by droughts, floods, pestilence, or even terrorists if it were being grown on millions upon millions of family farms rather than upon a few thousand mega farms? Smaller family farms could be modernized and even provided with a reasonable amount of fluff.

While not going into all the possible scenarios of how mega farming could fail, wouldn't it be ironic if they did fail sometime in the future and all the urban and city dwellers returned to small family farms to have access to the basics of survival? Today we're experiencing a new urban phenomenon called support your local food suppliers. With the increased suspicion of mega farms turning out potentially unhealthy food laced with harmful pathogens and heavy chemical fertilizers, many urban families are increasingly turning to locally grown foods and meats produced by growers they have become personally acquainted with. They can scrutinize how and where and under what conditions their food is being grown. This is being preferred, even if the locally grown food is more costly. Are we already going back to the era of small farms?

December 10, 2014

Hi, Tim,

I hope this finds you in good spirits and you are doing well. We enjoyed seeing you over Thanksgiving, and it was great to be with you. In this letter, I will introduce you to the children of Jonny and Vora.

The children: first born, John Jr., was born in 1921, then James in 1923, Frances in 1926, Vera in 1930, Fred in 1933, and the twins, Lois and Louis, in 1936.

It was almost like two separate families. By the time the twins were five years old, the three older children were no longer on the farm. Vera was like the buffer child between the older and younger children. Although not witnessing first-hand the childhood of the three older children, much of their childhood experiences were shared over the fifty plus years our close family spent together.

John Jr. was born at the height of prosperity for this small mining town. The town had grown from approx-imately 500 when it was first founded in about 1881 to approximately 2,500 in 1921. There was steady income from growing cotton, coal mining, and timbering. The coal mining companies built housing to accommodate the steady influx of men arriving to work in the coal mines. The coal in this region was of very good quality and was well suited for the fledging iron and steel industries springing up only sixty miles away in Birmingham. A branch of the Frisco railroad company passed through the small town and transported the cotton, coal, and timber to various markets.

As John Jr. and James were only sixteen months apart in age, they often told of their childhood days together working on the family farm. John Jr. was very even tempered, full of fun, and as the older brother, a very good protector and advisor for his younger brothers and sisters. He was almost like a father to the youngest children as they grew up. He handled this role well throughout his life. On the other hand, James was fierier in temperament. He could be easily provoked and engaged in several physical altercations during his teen years. During the Great Depression, 1929 to 1940, some enterprising feed and fertilizer companies began selling their hog and cow feed as well as fertilizer in good-quality, printed cotton sacks. These sacks were quite large as they contained one hundred pounds of feed or fertilizer. The brightly colored print on these rather large sacks could be unraveled at the seams and then utilized by rural housewives like Vora to make dresses for the girls and shirts for the boys. This probably would have been a great selling feature and very beneficial to the rural folks except for one thing: the snobbish city kids would tease and make fun of those feed sack dresses.

Vera told of an incident involving a feed sack dress. She stated that Vora had made a really pretty dress for Frances from the feed sacks. Vera told how very proud Frances was of her new dress as she went to school that morning. They met up with other children on the way to school and a snobbish city boy began teasing Frances and stated, "You want people to think you're wearing a store bought dress, but I know better, that's a feed sack dress!" Vera told how hurtful this was to Frances and she began to cry from this teasing. Vera then told James about this incident. After school that afternoon, James was waiting for this boy and according to Vera, "James gave him a good whipping!"

As soon as John Jr. and James were able to handle a team of horses, Jonny leased more bottom land to grow corn and cotton. During planting time, they were both taken out of school until the crops were planted. This was a common practice for all the rural families and the schools considered this as legitimate absences. The boys would be up at daylight, eat their breakfast, and then go out to the barn to hitch the team of mules. One mule was hitched to the wagon and the other was tied by his reins to the back of the wagon. They would load whatever farm equipment they would need into the wagon then get the lunch and water Vora had packed for them and head off to the bottom land. This was a trek of about three miles. Farming with horses or mules was very time consuming. Approximately three or four acres of land was all that could be turned in a day. Preparing and planting the corn and cotton required four different plowing operations. First the land had to be turned over. A turning plow was used to roll the sod over, turning it upside down so the fresh dirt was now on top. Sometimes if the plow struck a buried rock or tree root, it would cause the plow handle (called the plow stock) to whack the ribs of the one plowing very hard! This could happen over and over during the course of the day. The mule would need to be rested every half hour or even more often if it was very hot.

Once the land was turned, it was allowed to dry out for one or two days. Then a section harrow was used to break up the clods. A section harrow was about five feet wide with two rows of steel spikes which extended into the clods, smoothing and breaking then up into smaller lumps. Next, a drag was used to smooth out the ground into a smooth seed bed. The drag was simply a log approximately eight to ten inches in diameter and about ten feet long. Once the drag had sufficiently smoothed the soil, it was then ready to have the rows laid off. Jonny usually did this because he liked the rows straight and evenly spaced about three feet apart. Laying off the rows required a smaller plow which would open a furrow about three inches deep. Once all this was completed, the planter would follow the furrow, dropping the seeds, distributing the fertilizer, and covering and compacting the seeds into the soil. The planter was also pulled by the mule. It was always amazing how cooperative the mules were with these operations. They knew what was expected of them and seemed to try very hard to do it right. Once all the corn and cotton was planted, it would be a matter of two weeks before the corn and cotton would sprout and emerge from the soil.

Now it was time to plant the large vegetable garden and the potato patches. Green beans, okra, tomatoes, turnip greens, collards, peas, Irish potatoes, and sweet potatoes were all planted in the garden very near the house. After the cotton and corn came up, it required at least two weedings by hand. Every child old enough to properly use a hoe, as well as Vora, would have the task of weeding the crops. Once the hoeing was done, the older boys would then use the mule and a sweep plow to clear out the weeds between the rows.

Within about two weeks, the crops would be ready to repeat this all over again. After about a month, the cotton and corn would be big enough so the weeds and grass would not hamper its growth. The vegetable garden had to be constantly weeded all summer long.

By the time John Jr. and James were teenagers, the country was in the middle of the Great Depression (1929 to

1940). Most of the industrial jobs and the coal mining jobs were lost. It was even more critical for the farm to be productive in order to provide the family with income and food. Being on the farm then was far better than living in town.

When John Jr. graduated from high school in 1939, there were no jobs to be found. Without money, there was no hope for going to college. One of Jonny's sisters and her family had moved to San Diego, California, several years earlier. Through letters exchanged between Vora and the sister, Nell Tinner, it seemed hopeful that John Jr. could get an apprenticeship job at one of the aircraft plants in San Diego. Jonny went to the bachelor farmer, Jim Delevicheo, and borrowed fifty dollars to send John Jr. to California by train. Fortunately, John Jr. was accepted into the apprenticeship program as a sheet metal fabrication worker. Typical for that era, relatives like Nell and her family took their nephew into their home during his apprenticeship.

In 1941, James also graduated from high school. The war against Nazi Germany was already raging in Europe, and the bombing of Pearl Harbor was just months away. Typical of young men of that era, James decided to volunteer for military duty. He and his cousin who lived only about two miles up the road decided they would join under the buddy system. Under this system, the buddies were promised they would be placed in the same company (this didn't happen). The cousin was Dugan Meyers. He was an outstanding football player for the local high school. High school football was very popular among the town's folks. Crowds of upward of one thousand people would turn out for those games. Later the new football field would be named the Dugan Meyers Field. Dugan was always in top gear. Whether playing football or in combat, he was out front leading the pack. Town folks said they weren't surprised when they got the news that Dugan had been killed in action after being in combat for only six weeks. It was reported Dugan's company was assigned the task of capturing a vital bridge controlled by Nazi Germany. Typically, when the order was given to attack, Dugan was the first to lead the charge and died in his first combat experience.

James was shipped out to Europe as well. He was placed in the Signal Corp. His job was to string communication cables from the front lines back to the command headquarters. He spoke very little about his war experiences when he came home. I can only recall a few of the horrific things he shared about his war experiences. Once he was stringing wires on utility poles in a town just seized from the Nazis. A German sniper began firing at him. In his haste to get off the pole, he slipped and fell, striking his back against the street curb. He was sent back to a hospital for about six weeks, and when he recovered sufficiently, he rejoined his company. James was in Belgium in December 1944 when the last major offensive by the Nazis (Battle of the Bulge) took place. During this offensive attack by the Germans, James and two other American soldiers were cut off from their company and spent three days hiding by day and sneaking by night before rejoining their own company. One of the three was hit in the face by a German bullet but survived.

James told once about his company camping along a river. Swollen and bloated bodies of dead German soldiers were floating down this river. As they floated by, some of the American soldiers began to shoot them and the swollen bodies would explode! As the war began to wind down in Europe by early spring 1945, James told how his company was loaded on a ship but not told where they were going. Everyone thought they were headed home. After about ten days, they spotted land and then recognized it to be the east coast of the United States. They thought they would dock very soon at an east coast port. The ship, however, kept sailing south. Soon the American coast disappeared, and they sailed another ten days before going through the Panama Canal. After being on the ship for three months, they finally arrived in Okinawa to fight in the war against Japan. Fortunately, the atomic bomb attack on mainland Japan in August 1945 ended the war soon after their arrival in Okinawa. The next boat ride brought them back home. James had returned earlier due to his injured back still disabling him.

With all that he had endured, James arrived back home amazingly well adjusted. As far as I could tell, there was no post combat stress disorder; just a young soldier very happy to be back on the family farm.

(I'm not finished with the children yet, there'll be more to come.)

The Children Continued

Hi Tim,

We look forward to seeing you up here for Christmas. Have a good day!

John Jr. had done well in California. He had finished his apprenticeship and had purchased a fairly new car (a 1940 Ford coupe). I'm not sure why he decided to join the navy. I suspect it was patriotism, a willingness and desire to join in the fight to defend our country. Whatever the motivation, John Jr. left California and returned to the family farm. He built a storage shed for his car and then joined the navy. Ironically, after joining the navy, they recognized his skilled trade background and sent him right back to the San Diego Naval Base. There he worked on all the war damaged airplanes and ships sent there for repairs. He remained there and never left the United States during the war. Later he seemed to regret not being shipped overseas during the war. His skills in helping repair the damaged airplanes and ships, however, were a vital contribution to the war effort.

When the GI's were discharged from their military duty, the government provided six months of what James called rocking chair money. He had a regular check which came every two weeks. James was discharged prior to the end of the war due to his back injury. He arrived back on the farm about six months before the war with Japan officially ended. He suffered from this back injury the rest of his life. James remained on the farm about six to eight months after returning home from the war. John Jr. permitted James to use the Ford coupe until he was discharged from the navy and returned home. It was about midsummer in 1945 when James returned. Apparently the GI grub had a greater variety than what we had on the farm. The field peas were producing in abundance at midsummer. Vora utilized these black eyed peas daily at the noon and evening meal.

After all he had been through, James still had a sense of humor. One early morning, James came to the breakfast table still looking very sleepy. He sat down at the table and with a sleepy voice he blurted, "Pass the black eyed peas please!" While having the black eyed peas daily for noon and evening meals, we never got desperate that we needed to have them for breakfast. I'm sure some of our neighbors would have welcomed even black eyed peas for breakfast.

One day a playmate of Louis, Frank Hendrix, invited him to spend the night. The next morning, Frank's mother gave them a slice of tomato with some white gravy on it. That was all they had to eat. Louis had never eaten tomatoes for breakfast before, but it was good with the gravy on it.

During his time back home, James would spend time on the front porch playing checkers with Fred. Fred was about twelve years old and a master at playing checkers. Usually, right after breakfast, James would get the checkerboard out and set it up on the front porch. Fred would beat him every game. One morning, after losing three or four games to Fred, James thought he had Fred beaten. He was very confident he was about to win a game! Then he made a bad move and Fred beat him again! James grabbed up the checker board, with the checkers still on it, and threw it out into the yard! After James had cooled off the next day, he retrieved the checkerboard and continued to challenge Fred to play checkers. (I don't think he ever won, but nobody else ever did either when they played with Fred.)

One morning, the newspaper arrived and it had a large advertisement about a rodeo coming to Bingham. It had a picture of cowboys riding wild bulls and roping steers. The children asked James if he would take them to see the rodeo. James didn't say no but said if his rocking chair check came in time, maybe, just maybe, he would take them. The twins checked the mailbox every day hoping that check would come. Finally it did arrive, and true to word, James piled all the kids into the Ford coupe and took them to the rodeo. It was an all-day trip and a wonderful day. What a great older brother the children had!

On August 15, 1945, as usual, Vora was listening to the news on the radio when the newster announced that Japan had surrendered and the war was over! Vora began to weep with tears of joy. James began to yell and jump up and down. Soon all the children were jumping and shouting. James shouted, "Get in the car kids, we're going into town to celebrate." Once we got into town, James began to blow the car horn, and the kids had the windows down and were yelling out the windows. Suddenly a police car pulled up beside James while he was stopped at a traffic light. James looked over at the policeman and asked, "Do you mind? The policeman responded, "Hell no!" Soon a parade of cars was following us, honking horns and shouting out the windows. People began coming out of houses and shooting guns up in the air. How very grateful everyone was to hear that wonderful news! I don't really know how many young Walker

County men lost their lives in the war, but there were many who made the supreme sacrifice for their country.

Soon after VJ Day (August 15, 1945), John Jr. was discharged from the military and he came back to the family farm as well. He and James would sometimes scuffle and get into wrestling matches inside the house (all in fun) just as they had done as teenagers. Jonny still didn't tolerate it. He would yell at them, "You better behave because you're not too old that I won't take a belt to you!" John and James would giggle at that threat, but out of respect for their Pa, they would stop horsing around.

Soon after both boys were home, they took advantage of the GI bill which offered to pay their way through college. They both enrolled at Auburn University. They both chose vocational agriculture as their curriculum. Most weekends they came home as they had girlfriends in Walker County. They began to tell Jonny about all the new innovations in farming. They told him it was not advisable to use the deep turning plow which would hill the corn up and leave a deep furrow in the middle of the rows. They stated the deep turning damaged the root system of the corn and also made it more susceptible to drought by being mound up instead of on level ground.

Jonny would say, "I ain't interested in these newfangled ideas." He never changed his way of farming. Both John and James married while still attending college. Amazingly they found housing in a former prison camp near Auburn in the town of Opelika, Alabama. This was a former prison camp which held captured German prisoners during the war. Now the prison barracks were serving as housing for America heroes who enrolled in college. Both John Jr. and James graduated from Auburn University.

Frances was a very quiet, pleasant, and sweet girl. Vora would tell how the older boys would harass and tease Frances and Vera. Sometimes the boys would slip up behind the girls and place a praying mantis or a big green katydid on the girls' shoulders. The girls would scream and run to their mother to get it knocked off. Sometimes one of the boys would hold the girl while the other would pretend to nail shoes on her feet like they were shoeing a horse. Frances would tease the twins about how many diapers she had to change when they were babies. Much of the care for the twins was done by Frances and Vera. Frances loved to hug and play with the twins. Since the twins were only about six years old when Frances left home, most of the memories of her are when she would come home to visit. She left home right after graduating from high school and began working in a large department store in Birmingham. As was the custom then, if you had relatives in the area, you were invited to live with them until you could get your own place. Frances lived with one of Vora's younger sisters in Birmingham.

Within a year of being in Birmingham, Frances met a young man just returning home from the war. He was very similar in personality to Frances. He was quiet and had a very pleasant smile. Frances brought James Eason to the farm in order to meet Vora and Jonny. The first time the twins met James, Louis was in bed with a very bad case of mumps. Frances brought James into the front room where Louis was in bed. (Vora kept a spare bed in the front bedroom so a sick child could be more easily attended to during the night.) James Eason obviously felt very sorry for Louis and stated, "Poor Bubba!"

That weekend, he named Lois "Sissy" and Louis "Bubba." From that time forward, the twins were called Sissy and Bubba by James and Frances. Once Frances and James were married, they would come to the farm often to visit. They devoted much of their visit to playing with the twins. Usually they would bring treats or new clothing for the twins. During the summer months, James and Frances would take the twins home with them for about two weeks. The twins enjoyed their visits, and when they came home, Vora would say they were very spoiled! Like John Jr. and James Elliott, James Eason took advantage of the GI bill and went to college at Abilene Christian College in Texas. He graduated in 1952.

In the early 1930s, the boll weevil invaded the cotton crops in Alabama and Mississippi. This insect migrated out of Mexico and devastated the cotton farms in the United States. Before this invasion, cotton was called the King of the South. Prior to this invasion, Jonny had grown cotton in the bottom land. The cotton stalks would form numerous buds quite similar to a very small rose bud. These buds, or bolls as they were called, were what produced the cotton. The boll weevil would lay eggs on this boll and the larva would hatch and eat the boll as food. The boll would then fall off, and there would be no cotton produced from this plant. The cotton harvest was drastically reduced over the next decade. Cotton was no longer King of the South.

Due to numerous crop failures, Jonny stopped trying to grow cotton around 1943. There was a cotton gin near the railroad in the small town. The gin would separate the cotton seeds from the fiber. In late fall when the gin was operating, the whole town would be covered in very fine cotton fibers. It looked like a light snow even though the temperature was ninety degrees! Farmers would add tall side boards to their wagons and the wagons would be filled and overflowing with the cotton, but it was so light and fluffy it was easily pulled by the horses It was a common sight to see several horse and wagons lined up along the road waiting their turn to be unloaded. By this time, there were also trucks which hauled the cotton to the gin. In late fall, many cotton farmers would hire additional hands to help pick the cotton. The going rate was about two dollars per hundred pounds of cotton.

At about age twelve, Louis decided he would earn some money by picking cotton. The farmer gave him a long cotton picking sack with a shoulder strap on it. The cotton sacks were usually about eight feet long and were dragged along the row of cotton as the cotton fibers were pulled by hand from the plants. After picking all day, Louis took his bag to be weighed and receive his pay. He had picked only about 25 pounds of cotton and received forty cents for his day's labor! Some very fast cotton pickers could pick over two hundred pounds per day. A few years later, these hand pickers were replaced by mechanized cotton harvesters. A cotton field ready to be picked looks like a field covered with snow.

Once Vera, Fred, Lois, and Louis were weeding a field of cotton up near the house. Somehow Louis provoked Fred, and Fred raised his hoe above his head and charged toward Louis. Fortunately Louis was a fast runner and dropped his hoe and ran toward the house. Fred seemed to be gaining on Louis when suddenly Vera caught up with Fred and made a flying tackle from behind! Vera sat on Fred until he cooled off enough, so it would be safe to let him up.

The fourth child, Vera, was somewhat of a tomboy. She enjoyed exploring in the woods and fields, but she was also very much a young lady. She enjoyed pretty dresses and primping in front of a mirror. She was small, perky, and attractive. One day when she was about fourteen years old, Vora sent her out to the wood pile to split kindling wood for the next morning's fires. A young man came up the trail which came right through the yard. He saw Vera splitting the wood and asked her if she would like him to help her. Vera agreed and Garland assisted her with the chore. He explained that he was on leave from the army and was going to see his uncle, Dewy Hendrix, who lived about a mile up the road. He told Vera he was about to be shipped overseas and asked Vera if she would write to him. Vera stated she would if it was okay with her mother.

Vora agreed that Vera could write to Garland, and she corresponded with Garland all during the war. When Vera was in the eleventh and twelfth grades, she was selected with three other girls to be majorettes. She and the other three would lead the band onto the field at the beginning of the football games. They would also perform during halftime with the band. These girls were very attractive and also very popular in school. Sometimes these girls would come over to the farm, and they would practice their marching routines. I dare say Fred and Louis gave them admiring stares as they performed in their little short skirts and fancy boots!

Sometime after the war was over, that soldier boy came back up the trail and knocked at the door. Vera had just graduated from high school, and it wasn't long before Garland asked her to marry him. It didn't take Vera long to say yes. After they were married, Vera and Garland moved to Adamsville, Alabama, and he took a job as a truck driver hauling coal from a huge strip mine near Graysville, Alabama. After about three years, Garland decided he would also go to college by utilizing the GI bill. Both he and Vera enrolled at Jacksonville State Teacher's college in Alabama. Both Garland and Vera graduated with teaching degrees. Like James, Garland had experienced many horrific things during the war. He had fought in France and Germany. He also discussed very little about his war experiences.

The fifth child, Fred, was intelligent and an excellent student but chose all his life to play the role of a country bumpkin. He possessed a rare talent for making people laugh. He is a Will Rogers, Andy Taylor, and Gomer Pyle all rolled into one. He probably would have become rich and famous had he chosen to be a stand-up comedian for his vocation. Like James, Fred had a fiery side to his personality. He engaged in numerous fisticuffs during his teenage years. Unfortunately, during Fred's junior and senior high school years, he began to experience seizures. These seizures became progressively worse during his senior year in school. Fred had to stay home and much of his schooling was done by having the twins bring homework home for him to complete. The next day, the twins would return the completed work to his teachers.

Even though Fred was absent from school most of his senior year, he graduated first in his class and was the valedictorian. Jonny and Vora had taken Fred to almost every doctor in Walker County seeking treatment for his seizures. All the medications they prescribed were ineffective. Once Vora noticed an advertisement in a magazine about medication for seizures and she sent away for it. Even though it was not prescribed by a doctor, it seemed to work and the seizures went away and never returned. Some skeptics say it was just growing pains and Fred simply outgrew the malady.

When Fred graduated from high school, he was accepted in an apprenticeship program at the Redstone Arsenal in Huntsville, Alabama. This is where the government did most of their research and development in rocket science. Due to the Korean conflict, Fred was drafted into the army in 1952. He was sent to Germany instead of Korea. This was during the time Berlin was divided by the wall the Russians built to divide Berlin into an east and west zone. Once he returned from his military duty, Fred returned to his job at the Redstone Arsenal. He worked there for twenty-five years before retiring.

Fred once stated that he had moved so many times while living in North Alabama that his washer and dryer had one hundred thousand miles on them! One time, he had all his household goods on an old trailer while he was moving to a new location, a junk man pulled up beside him and yelled, "Fellow, if you're taking that to the dump, I'll take it off your hands." Fred yelled back, "Man, this ain't junk, it's my furniture!"

One of his jobs at the Arsenal was attaching rocket launchers to the bellies of helicopters that were being used in Vietnam. Once attached, the pilots would then fly the helicopters down range and test fire the rockets. One day, just after Fred had completed attaching the rocket launchers, the pilot invited Fred to ride with him in the helicopter while he test firing the rockets. Fred replied, "No way, I know who worked on that thing!"

We've explained how Vora would make dresses for the girls or shirts for the boys from printed fertilizer sacks. These sacks would have the chemical composition printed in soluble ink which would easily wash off. Numerals such as 6-8-4 or 12-12-12 or 6-8-10 would be on the sack, designating the percentage of nitrogen, phosphorus, and potash in the fertilizer. Fred stated that when he went to the store to buy his very first store-bought shirt, the store clerk asked him what size he wore. He said, "I'm not for sure. The last one my mother made for me was size 6-8-4."

He often complained that his right hind leg was bothering him! Anytime a family reunion was being planned, it was guaranteed to be a great time if they knew Fred planned to be there.

The sixth child, Lois, was a beautiful baby and she never outgrew that loveliness. She was a natural beauty with blonde curly hair, deep blue eyes, and was a cutie from head to toe. She was selected as most beautiful for the senior year-book. She and Louis were twins but shared very few physical attributes. Louis had a dark completion, very dark hair, dark brown eyes, and until junior high, Lois was always about a head taller than Louis. Due to sharing the same birthday, however, they were always close. They seldom argued or had disagreements. The only thing annoying to Louis was being put on display by Vora at annual gatherings for decoration days at the cemeteries, family reunions, or funerals. The relatives and friends of Vora and Jonny would always want to see the twins. Vora would gladly oblige. She would stand the twins side by side in front of her for everyone to gawk at. Then the folks would always say, "Why, Vora, they don't look a thing alike!" Louis would always think, "Well, duh, she's a girl and I'm a boy!"

Many boys sought to woo Lois. One method many of them would use was to pretend to be a friend of Louis. Louis easily saw through this hypocrisy and never befriended such. While very popular in junior and high school, Lois set the standards pretty high for those she would date. Her high moral standards and religious convictions reduced the number of would-be suitors significantly. She never had a serious relationship with any high school classmates even though many tried and there were many broken hearts.

When Lois was sixteen years old, she went down to Vera and Garlands for the summer and found a job in a department store in Jacksonville, Alabama. She hoped to earn some money for the extra expenses anticipated for her senior year in high school. While there, she met the man of her dreams. Bobby Duncan had just finished high school and was preparing to leave for college that fall and attend Freed Hardeman College in Henderson, Tennessee. When Lois visited the church where Bobby attended, he was smitten! Since he had all the credentials Lois had in mind for a boyfriend, they spent the summer together getting to know one another, and by fall when they had to separate, they both were very much in love.

During her senior year in high school, there was rarely a weekend when Bobby didn't come to see her. After all, the family farm was right on the route from Jacksonville, Alabama to Henderson, Tennessee. (What's 150 miles out of the way if you're in love?) Lois and Bobby were married in the fall of 1954.

Sequel

In recent years, there has been a growing concern about obesity among our children in the United States. According to one article written in 2012, approximately one-third of American children are overweight or are at risk of becoming overweight. We have seen this number more than double in the past thirty years. Thinking back to the 1930 to '40s, during the depression years, obesity was all but nonexistent among American children. I can recall only two teenage girls (from the same family) that I considered overweight among the approximate fifty children in our rural community. As a matter of fact, most of the children back then were on the thin side. Today children are being encouraged to reconsider their diet and food choices in order to combat this growing trend. Proper diet and exercise are being promoted in our schools and by the government. Fast foods, fatty foods, sugary soda pop, and mountains of french fries are not easily abandoned once the taste for such is acquired.

In today's teenage world, it's a challenge to find the time for exercise. There's so much TV watching, Internet exploring, texting, and just hanging out at the malls that it's difficult to find time to exercise. Back in depression days, children's diet in rural America consisted primarily of home-grown turnip greens, collard greens, green beans, tomatoes, potatoes, and fresh fruits All these rank at the top as the most nutritious among all foods. They are rich in vitamins, minerals, fiber, and low in cholesterol and calories. There were no sugary drinks, just raw whole milk loaded with good bacteria needed for good digestion and probiotics which promotes good absorption of certain hard to digest foods. These ingredients are not in pasteurized milk or cheese. Today you can only get these ingredients in natural yogurt or by swallowing pills! Of course there's a risk to drinking raw milk if the source is unsanitary, but it is generally accepted that the risk of transmitting a disease is low if proper management of the herd and handling of the raw milk is practiced.

Beef was rarely eaten (too expensive). And we know today that excessive consumption of red meat is considered to be a strong contributing factor leading to heart disease and cancer. Protein from meat was eaten in moderation due to the cost and accessibility. Meats in general were limited. Chicken and wild meat, like rabbits and squirrels, as well as pork were eaten in small portions. The mother would prepare the children's plate. One piece of chicken or one slice of pork roast was placed on each child's plate, and when each child had received a portion, then the plate would be filled with ample portions of turnip greens, green beans, potatoes, etc., and the plate would be cleaned up! Maybe past generations were blessed and didn't know it when not permitted to indulge in excessive eating.

Principle diet of depression era children:	Calories
Turnip, mustard, collard greens: high in fiber, minerals, vitamins	60 per serving
Black eyed peas: high in minerals, vitamins, fiber, protein	40
Sweet potatoes: rich in minerals, vitamins, fiber	110
Chicken or pork roast: high in protein, minerals, iron	160
White potatoes: rich in vitamins A, C, B, minerals, fiber	160
Tomatoes: rich in trace minerals and vitamins, betaine	80
	Total: 610

Principle diet today	
Big Mac: 296 g fat, 75 g cholesterol	550
French fries (large): 250 g fat, 2.2 g saturated fat	578
One slice of pizza: saturated fat	184
	Total: 1,309

Another factor distinguishing past generations of children from today's children is the difference in the amount of physical exercise or work. We walked everywhere. Two miles away, we walked; five miles away, we walked or rode a bike; ten miles away, we walked or rode a bike. Once when I was sixteen years old, I walked twenty miles to a store (it took me about three hours). Fortunately, I was lucky enough to hitch a ride back home! Most of the walking was either uphill or downhill. Downhill was great on a bike but very tough coming back and peddling uphill. I broke many bicycle chains trying to pedal a bicycle up a steep grade! Weeding acres of cotton and corn were also major sources of physical exercise. Rural depression era children looked forward to Sundays when we didn't have to work in the fields. Once back from church, we had the rest of the day off to play. And how did we play? Racing each other, playing hide and seek for hours, or playing a game of football or walking to a friend's house. Just sitting around the house would have been a waste of playing time!

After World War II, the federal government offered free college tuition and housing allowance to returning GIs who wished to go to college or trade school. This was a wonderful program! Many took advantage of this opportunity. There's no doubt in my mind that this program returned huge dividends back to the government. These well-educated young men became leaders in industry, government, and education. Our government and institutions of higher learning today would be wise to take a look back at this program. Today many deserving young men and women are being denied opportunities for advancing their knowledge and training due to the very high cost of college tuition. It has been estimated that the typical college graduate today graduates from college with a student loan debt of approximately $150,000. They do not get this paid off until they're about forty years old!

Today many intelligent and academically qualified young high school graduates are not continuing their education simply because it isn't affordable for them. We need to find ways in our country to make higher education affordable for everyone who could benefit from it. For those qualifying and desiring to advance their education, there should be government programs such as the GI bill which was so successful after World War II. It was successful back then, so why not now?

Stay positive and have a great week. Will see you up here next week!

The Small Town

Hi Tim,

Sorry you were unable to make it up here for Christmas. We missed you and hope you're feeling better. It was difficult to find time to do any writing during the holidays. In this letter, I'd like to describe the small town and its people.

The destiny of the small town was determined eons ago when rich deposits of coal, limestone, and iron ore were all formed in a relatively close proximity to each other. Geologist and scientist theorize that the region, which is present-day Alabama, was once very near the equator. Lush tropical forest and swamps provided the organic matter which millions of years later was transformed into coal. The Appalachian Mountains were thought to be at one time as tall as the Alps or Rocky Mountains. Because this mountain chain is considered millions of years older, however, the Appalachians have eroded away to the point where its tallest peak is 6,684 feet high: Mt. Mitchell in North Carolina. Subsequent volcanic activity and the movement of the earth's tectonic plates created the enormous mountain range which stretches from the Canadian border all the way into North Central Alabama. The Appalachian mountain range was a natural barrier which kept the thirteen original colonies from moving westward for over one hundred years. Most of the area south of Virginia and South Carolina also remained unexplored until after 1812.

Most often we assume that the British influence and impact held over the American colonies ended with the Declaration of Independence in 1776. Not so! For the next thirty-six years, the dominating British navy played havoc with the colonies' commerce and shipping. The English would sink American merchant ships and commandeer the American sailors for their own ships. This detrimental impact of the British navy on the American colonies was not eliminated until the war of 1812 with the English fleet being decimated in the battle of Mobile Bay and New Orleans. The final chapter of England's desires and attempts to dominate American commerce and shipping ended. After the war of 1812 ended, there was a sizeable number of American military soldiers remaining in Mobile. The American government commissioned these soldiers to explore from Mobile Bay northward, hoping to discover a waterway suitable for shipping commerce from the middle of the state to Mobile and then on to Europe. Historians credit the discovery of vast deposits of iron ore, coal, and limestone to these military explorers.

According to Wikipedia, Major Jonathan Mayhan is generally credited with the discovery of these vast deposits of minerals in this region. Major Mayhan and some of the other soldiers remained in the area for several years. Some married Native American Indian women. The most dominant Indian tribes were the Choctaws, Cherokees, Creeks, and Tuskegee tribes. While failing to find a suitable waterway for commercial shipping to Mobile Bay, the discovery of these vast deposits of minerals would eventually lead to the settlement and development of the iron industry in Birmingham in 1871. Numerous small towns began to spring up and mine the coal necessary to supply the energy needed to smelt the iron ore. The first commercial operations of coal mining began in Walker County in 1856.

In 1889, the Frisco Railroad Company built a railroad line from Birmingham, Alabama to Memphis, Tennessee, with a spur line extending to Kansas City, Missouri. With these three elements in place—the high quality iron ore in Birmingham, the deposits of coal and limestone nearby, and now the railroad supplying the transportation—there became a demand for workers in the area. Emigrants from Scotland, Ireland, and Wales, as well as Americans from other regions of the country, came seeking work. The Federal Government encouraged this migration to this remote region by offering homestead land for sale at the rate of $1.25 per acre! Jonny's dad was among these emigrants from England.

In the region south of Walker County was a large delta plain of very fertile black soil which stretched across the entire state of Alabama. This delta, or grassy plain, was very suited for growing cotton. It was called the black belt' because of the very dark color of the rich soil. This area had been developed into cotton plantations by the late 1700s. Large numbers of slaves were brought to the area to supply the labor needed to grow the cotton and tobacco. These slaves were not imported from Africa but rather they were brought to this region from Maryland, Virginia and the Carolinas. After the war of 1812 ended, these slaves comprised over 50 percent of the black belt population. Cotton became the chief agricultural crop of this area and most of the cotton was exported from Mobile Bay to Europe. After these slaves were freed by the Emancipation Proclamation in 1863, they began to migrate north into Walker County, seeking work in the coal mines. The invention of the cotton gin in 1793 and a decrease in demand for cotton resulted in these illiterate freemen to no longer be in high demand in the cotton industry. Since the coal mining industry was expanding in the region of north central Alabama, many of these former slaves and the children of former slaves migrated from the cotton plantations to the coal mines. Within a short time, the freemen comprised approximately half of the mine workers. The small Walker County town was settled in 1888. By the turn of the century, the small town had grown to a population of over 2,500 people. The Galloway Coal Co. became the most prominent coal company. The Galloway Company employed approximately 2,000 workers and began building row houses for the workers. One such housing located very near No. 11 mines was called Bynum Camp. This camp was located approximately one mile outside the small town. All the mine entrances were identified by a number. Sometimes a road near the mine would also be designated as a number. For example, a road near No. 11 mine was also referred to as No. 11 Hill.

The small town extended east to west for approximately one mile along the main east-west road. The road ran parallel with the Frisco railroad. The Front Street, as it was called, had a number of businesses which sprang up very quickly. A hardware store, drug store, boot shop, hotel, clothing store, and even a pool hall were built adjoining one another along the street. Each business had a rear door which opened into a large alleyway where the horses and wagons were tied while the rural folks did their shopping on Saturdays. Of course the Galloway Coal Co. had their own store. Much of the miner's pay was in script money, which would only be accepted at the company store. Tennessee Ernie Ford, a famous country and western singer during the '50s and the '60s had a very popular song he recorded which states:

Some people say a man is made out of mud
A poor man is made out of muscle and blood
Muscle and blood and skin and bone
A mind that's weak and a back that's strong
You load sixteen tons and what do you get?
Another day older and deeper in debt
St. Peter, don't you call me 'cause I can't go
I owe my soul to the company store!

Col. Robert Galloway, of Scottish descent, came from Memphis, Tennessee, in 1890 and purchased the coal mining rights from the Kansas City Coal and Coke company for $130,000. Perhaps being an astute business man of his days, or perhaps just due to greed, the miners were treated very unjustly. Wages were low, safety hazards were numerous, and many were killed due to explosions and cave-ins. Unrest among the miners began to surface. There was strong competition between the white miners and the arriving freemen (former slaves) for the jobs. Racial tension grew, and some houses in the Negro quarters were burned. Tension escalated to the point where some Negroes and whites were murdered. Further tension came from the fact that the State Militia was called in and promptly sided with the Galloway superintendent who discharged approximately two hundred white miners which Galloway deemed to be troublemakers. Further complications developed due to the fact that the State Government had a "lease" program whereby convict or prisoners could be leased to the mine owners for thirty-five cents per day.

These convicts were harshly treated and received no wages for their labor. Most of these convicts were former slaves and were not guilty of any crimes! Both white and Negro miners began to try to unionize. The management of the Galloway Coal Co., determining to crush the union attempt, brought in more "freemen" to replace the striking miners. They sought to eliminate all those they deemed to be troublemakers. With the support of the State Militia, arrests were being made that resulted in the Militia killing two white miners and the miners retaliating by killing a Militia man. The attempt to unionize was broken until 1920 when John L. Lewis, president of the United Mine Workers of America, called for a state-wide strike of Alabama mine workers. By 1920, the demand for coal had declined and competition from other states again caused the balance of power to be with the coal companies, resulting once again in the miners being unable to unionize. Miners continued to be poorly paid and endure harsh working conditions until they were finally able to unionize nationally in the 1950s.

As the small town grew, the merchants, mine management and engineers, lawyers, doctors, and railroad employees began to build homes directly north of the small town on the gently sloping hill which ascended from the main street. Several very large antebellum-style homes were constructed on large stately and beautifully landscaped lots. Many of the homes were later occupied by children and grandchildren of these former owners. In more recent years, almost all these homes have either been destroyed by fires, tornadoes, or have been abandoned and allowed to just rot away.

The main street of the small town was approximately on mile long, stretching east to west along the main road. On the east end of the town were Negro quarters comprised of approximately thirty crudely constructed houses. These houses were built of slab wood (waste wood collected from sawmills) with rusty tin roofs. Most were supported with log pillars which raised them about two feet off the ground. They were no better than former slave quarters. Another

Negro quarters was located on the extreme western side of the small town. These homes were better constructed, were larger, and made with milled wood siding. Most still remained unpainted. Ma Rosie and Pa Jim's house was right at the demarcation line between the white community and the Negro community. There was a parcel of land approximately fifty feet wide which separated the white community from the Negro community. The Negro family directly across the demarcation line from Ma Rosie and Pa Jim were named Lucy and James.

Lucy and James's house had a small front porch facing south just like Ma Rosie's and Pa Jim's house. Oftentimes, while visiting with Ma Rosie, we would carry on conversations with Lucy across the demarcation line. Lucy was always careful to address the white folks very humbly and respectfully. She would sometimes ask us to bring her some milk and butter when we brought it to Ma Rosie. In 1926, a Negro school was built on the east side of the small town within the boundaries of the Negro quarters. It was built of wood and always appeared to be poorly maintained.

The children of the small town professionals had their own unique speech and mannerisms. They tended to socialize with each other at school and spoke gracefully and with dignity. They tended to soften harsh words while overemphasizing gracious words. Their speech was patterned after the ole South cities such as Atlanta, Memphis, and Charlotte. On the other hand, the rural children coming to school brought with them the frontier dialect of a Daniel Boone or Southern redneck. The notable difference in the language was a challenge for the teachers. They were always correcting the rural children's vocabulary and pronunciation. Add to this mix the Negro dialect, and it became difficult at times to communicate!

I heard it might rain today. (City children)
I heered it's gunna rain today. (Rural children)
I done bees hear it gwina rain. (Negro)

Hello there, you all. (City children)
Howdy yawl. (Rural children)
Hey dar. (Negro)

Are you going to the store? (City children)
Air you 'ens going to the stow? (Rural children)
Does yo bees gwine to the stow? (Negro)

During the prosperous years from 1890 until about 1925, the small town grew rapidly. It was a rough and tough small town with heavy drinking and brawling taking place each payday. There was much hostility among the various ethnic groups who came to work in the mines. Miners also continued to squabble with the mine owners over wages and working conditions. These tough miners had little respect for local law enforcement. Whenever there was trouble, the sheriff usually couldn't be found.

After 1925, there was a substantial drop in demand for Walker County coal. The First World War had ended in 1918, and there was less demand for coal for war use. The high quality iron ore around Birmingham had been exhausted, and the country in general was approaching the Great Depression of 1929. Most of the larger underground mines had closed down. People began to move away from the small town. Stores along the main street were beginning to be boarded up. The only remaining mines were small privately operated mines which supplied the local demands for coal. These mines were called push mines and usually employed three to five workers. One such mine owner was referred to by Jonny as Ole Man Taylor'. Fortunately, Mr. Taylor kept Jonny employed as much as he could, and Jonny worked for Mr. Taylor two to three days a week The mines were referred to as push mines because each miner would load his own assigned coal car in the mines and then manually push the car out of the mines to the tipple where it was weighed before being unloaded. Each miner was paid according to the total weight of coal he pushed out each day. The coal cars were pushed along steel tracks installed on the floor of the mine tunnels.

Numerous small merchants struggled to stay in business, but slowly, more and more of them closed. From 1929 until 1941, the Great Depression held a strangle hold on the entire country. Homeless people could be seen daily as they rode the empty railroad cars through the small town. Some begged for food from the remaining stores still open. After dark, some would slip out of town and raid the rural farms, stealing chickens, eggs, or anything else they could find. Even though it was a challenge for Vora and Jonny to keep their own family clothed and fed, Vora would frequently prepare a plate of food for these homeless people. They were not called homeless but rather referred to as hobos. Food was also shared with other relatives and friends. Some relatives were reluctant to accept handouts but would come and help with harvesting the corn or help with the haying and then sit down at the dinner table with dignity and consume an enormous amount of food.

In 1933, Franklin Roosevelt was elected president of the United States. Most historians credit Roosevelt for pulling the country out of the depression. Certainly, the beginning of World War II in 1941 created a huge demands for jobs and was a major contributing factor as well. In 1935, Roosevelt enacted legislation which created the New Deal. The program called the Work Progress Administration allowed local governments of towns to apply for grants to improve their infrastructures. This program was usually referred to simply as the WPA (some critics of the program referred to it as "We Piddle Around" program). The small town was blessed with some very wise and shrewd town officials who applied for a federal grant. They speculated that if they didn't do anything, the town would be abandoned soon and resort to a ghost town. Hence they applied and were awarded a federal grant of $182,000 in 1937. In very short order, approximately 25 percent of the jobs held by the residents of the small town were jobs created by utilizing this grant money. A new high school and post office were built. Improvements were made to other schools and even churches. Streets were paved, sidewalks and curbs added, a water treatment plant was built, and sanitary sewers were installed. Even a new football field and a swimming pool were built. Most importantly, this grant created several hundred good paying and desperately needed jobs.

However, this was only a temporary fix. More needed to be done to pull the small town out of its downward spiral. Efforts were made to attract other diverse industries to the town, but nothing significant became of this. Only the lumber industry and paper mills continued to provide employment for some local residents. The small town continued to decline until the beginning of World War II in 1941. A renewed demand for coal saw the mining operations start up again. However, a new mining technique called strip mining was being utilized instead of the underground tunnels. Huge bulldozers and giant shovels were now being used to strip the dirt and rock off the top of the coal seams which were close to the surface. This produces large quantities of coal but does not require nearly as many employees. This process is still being utilized in Walker County today.

The small town continues to hang on but has become more or less a retirement community for senior citizens and a bedroom community for younger workers who live there but commute to Birmingham, Florence, Huntsville, and Decatur for employment. Perhaps the final decisive blow came to the small town recently when a new expressway was constructed about five miles north of the town. This expressway has reduced traffic through the town to just a trickle of local traffic. More stores are being boarded up and the census has shown a steady decline since 2000.

Sequel to follow. You have a very good week, Tim!

Sequel: The Small Town

Even during the very early colonial days in America, a form of slavery existed. Many of the early colonial industrialist practiced a form of slavery by utilizing the indentured servant programs. Generally, a young man eighteen to twenty-one years of age was selected to live and work with a master craftsman or skilled tradesman without being paid. In exchange for his labor, he was taught the trade by the master craftsman. This was for a prescribed period of time, usually ten years or less. The indentured servant was then permitted to leave and start his own business. Carpenters, stone masons, printers, blacksmiths, engravers, and carriage makers were some of the original trades which utilized young men as indentured servants. The problem with this program was that just when the young man became most profitable and skilled at his trade, he was free to leave and start his own business. This proved to be a poor investment for the master craftsman.

Once large scale farming of tobacco and cotton began, a great need was created for a large labor pool to grow and harvest these crops. Such large labor pools did not exist in Colonial America, hence the plantation owners turned to the purchasing of imported African slaves for their plantation laborers. Plantation owners rationalized that the African slaves were far better off on the American plantations than they were in primitive, undeveloped Africa. This was probably true from a purely physical environment, but never underestimate the value of freedom when it comes to assessing the quality of one's life. This initial utilization of slaves in Colonial America has created moral, ethical, and social issues which have plagued America for over 230 years.

Slavery was opposed by many prior to being introduced in America. The Civil War, at a huge cost, supposedly ended slavery but it didn't resolve moral and social issues associated with it.

Freed African slaves were not accepted as having full citizenship for another one hundred years. In the South, the policy of separate but equal failed. In the 1960s and '70s, Whites who fled to the suburbs proved very costly to inner cities. Mandated integration in the 1960s faced major opposition. White supremacy complicated matters. Black power and civil disobedience didn't help.

Presently, our nation still struggles with racial injustices; some very real, others perceived. In a random survey conducted in 2012, racial attitudes have not improved in America, even with the election of a black president. In 2008, the survey results indicated that 48 percent of Americans harbored some racial biases. In 2012, this same survey indicated 51 percent of Americans had racial biases.

Personally, I don't feel we need more surveys which tell us racial prejudices exist; we know that. But rather, we need a greater focus on determining why it exists and how do we resolve it? A Harvard professor of psychology suggested in an article that personal connections are a form of discrimination and prejudices practiced in our culture. She states that personal connections is a form of favoritism practiced in almost all aspects of American society. Bosses tend to hire those with whom they feel they have a personal connection. Families extend dinner invitations to those with whom they feel they have a personal connection. A senator is much more inclined to grant an interview with a reporter from his own hometown rather than others requesting interviews. People attend church services where they feel they have a personal connection. Professor Banasi cites an experience she had when she went to a hospital emergency room due to a severe glass cut on her hand. She was being treated very routinely by the emergency room staff until they discovered she was a Harvard professor. Once they were aware of her status, several specialist were called in, and the level of attention she was given elevated considerably.

The ghetto subculture with the hip-hop rap music, baggy clothing, hoodies, profanities, drugs, and street gangs makes it all but impossible for them to make personal connections with anyone outside their subculture. Stereotyping? I think not. The rural children in their bib overalls with patches on the knees were shunned by most of the city children in their fancy clothes and eloquent speech. Rural children were called hillbillies and country hicks by the city children. I never envied the city children because of their good fortune but rather felt that if they had a piece of the good life, then there was hope I could achieve it as well. With the encouragement of Vora to get a good education and Jonny instilling the value of hard work, the ingredients necessary for a successful life was implanted in their children early in life.

In my eleventh grade chemistry class, a good friend of mine (a city boy) sat directly behind me. He was very confused with the first semester's basic chemistry concepts. As we sat in the back of the room and could easily exchange whispers, he often got his test answers from me during that first semester. When the grades came out for that first semester, I was shocked to see a D for my grade. I knew I had done better and deserved a better grade than that. (This was the first and last time I ever received a D.) When I checked with the city boy about his grade, he informed me that he had gotten an A. He had a personal connection with the teacher. He lived near her in town. The remainder of the year, I received all As for my grades and the city boy was lucky to get a C- or D! (I quit whispering during the test.)

By my senior year, hard work and good grades began to pay dividends in school. I was selected as president of the honor society, had the leading role in the school play, and was voted Most Likely to Succeed by the school staff. I feel this still holds true today. In order to achieve success in life, hard work and a good education are of utmost importance and can overcome numerous obstacles. Why weren't these same values instilled in the Southern Black population after their freedom in 1863?

Some researchers remind us that the deplorable act of being regulated to the position of being a slave is so demoralizing that personal identity is totally lost. No heritage, no culture, no self-worth, no dignity, no trace of ancestry, and on and on we could go. As a result, once freed from slavery, the Southern Negro race began to find their self-worth through their own subculture. Negro spirituals were embraced in all Negro churches. Young thugs emerged as role models to be admired and emulated. Drug use and crime became acceptable ways to earn money in the ghetto. Should we blame young black men for engaging in antiestablishment social and criminal behavior, or should we blame our white society for regulating them to this hopeless lifestyle? Sadly, some 150 plus years after the Emancipation Proclamation, our culture still hasn't figured it all out!

Another professor has written a piece about the need for us to learn how to unlearn biases. Most of us, without even being aware, carry around inherited biases from our families or cultures which are often blatantly prejudice. How do we unlearn these prejudices? We tend to subconsciously carry these biases with us.

Blacks need to unlearn the bias that all prejudice against them is solely due to the color of their skin.

Blacks need to unlearn the bias that all white policemen are out to get them. Whites need to unlearn the bias that any black in a hoodie is a criminal.

Whites need to unlearn the bias that when blacks move into a neighborhood, the property values automatically go down.

Much progress has been made over my lifetime in improving racial inequalities. As a young child growing up in Alabama, I didn't recognized the blatant racial prejudices which existed in the South. That was just the way things were. I hadn't learned how to unlearn my inherited biases. Lucy and James determined the best recourse for them was to play the role of Uncle Tom and be polite, respectful, and courteous to the white folk. That's just the way it was and it seemed to work for them.

On the other hand, young black men and teenage boys were much more defiant. They were deeply disappointed that the Civil War had not truly liberated them. They weren't allowed to walk down the front street of the small town. They were required to enter the stores through the back ally doors. There were "white only" and "colored only" drinking fountains on the walls of the court houses (many times only a few feet apart). There was no interaction between white and black school-aged children. Upon graduating from high school in 1954, I never once had a child of color in my classes the entire twelve years. Teenage white boys didn't walk down the streets of the Negro quarters. They knew there would be trouble! Conversely, Negro teenage boys did not walk in white neighborhoods. As a young teenager, the only interactions I had with teenage Negro boys were confrontational ones. As a teenager, I never considered nor comprehended the wrongfulness of these prejudices. Now I can see how morally and socially wrong my childhood attitude was toward Negros. It was just the way things were. Thankfully through time my viewpoints have radically changed.

Progress has been slow, but for the most part, it has moved in a positive way. There are no states in the United States where blacks are in the majority.

Mississippi has the largest population of blacks, comprising 38 percent of their total population. Thirty one of our states have a black population of less than 10 percent.

Yet since 1967, nearly every major city in America has had a black mayor at one time or another. In the 1960s, there were only eight cities of any significant size in America with black mayors. In the 2000s, there has been forty-three black mayors elected in very significantly sized American cities. That's progress! From my personal experience of coming from the very worst of racial prejudices in the deep South during the '30s, '40s, and '50s to the conditions of 2015, I am grateful for all the achievements.

The Ridge Folks

Hi, Tim,

I hope you have a very, very good week!

From the extreme western end of the small town, a rural dirt road extends across the level valley floor southward, approximately one mile before crossing a bridge over a medium-sized creek and then proceeds to wind its way up a hill to the top. The hill is approximately six hundred feet tall, and the top has been eroded away through eons of time to form a relatively flat plateau comprised of several hundred acres of land. Much of this land is suitable for farming, and approximately one half of the home sites were situated on small farms. At the top of the hill, the road intersects with another road which extends east to west across the entire top of the plateau. The road then descends back down to the valley floor at each end. The flat plateau is approximately two miles long from its eastern to western limits. Due to the top being relatively flat, the ridge was very suitable for home sites all along the road. From the rim of the plateau, there was a commanding view of the small town in the valley below. The ridge people seemed oblivious to the beautiful view. Aesthetics was not a factor considered as to where the homes on the ridge were located. To the ridge children, however, the ridge provided a spectacular view of the night sky. Almost anytime you were outside at night you were in awe of the vastness of the heavens and the magnificent display of shooting stars.

Fifteen homes were located all along the east-west road. Within these homes there were approximately fifty children. Almost every home had six to eight children. The forest was overrun with free-range chickens and children! The children were permitted to roam and explore wherever they desired. Hardly any No Trespassing signs existed. All the homes were within walking distance from each other, and the children became close and much time was spent playing with all the neighborhood children. The old bachelor, Jim Delevicheo, was the only ridge person who would chase the children off his property.

Four of the fifteen homes were very old log-cabin-style construction. Most likely these log homes were constructed by early settlers who were the first to settle this region when the government was selling land for $1.25 per acre. All the log homes were almost identical in construction. The kitchen and sitting rooms were separated from the bedrooms by an open-ended, covered breezeway. People referred to the breezeway as the dog run since it was always open and the dogs often slept there. I suppose the breezeway provided a nice place to sit on very warm days.

As you came up the dirt road on the east end of the plateau, the first home you came upon was one of these log-cabin-style homes. The Inman family lived in this log home as well as Great-Grandpa Meyers. The Inmans, Shorty and Kitty, had seven children. All the girls slept in one bedroom and the boys slept in the other. Shorty and Kitty slept in the sitting room adjoining the kitchen. The log home had a large stone fireplace which used logs to heat the sitting room and kitchen area. Of course the children's bedrooms were unheated. On cold winter nights, it was nice to have bed partners so you could keep warm.

I'm sure Shorty had a given name, but I don't think any of the ridge people could tell you what it was! As his name implied, he was a very short man, perhaps about five feet and two inches tall. Shorty worked at the coal mine, but I don't think he worked in the tunnels. He worked at the tipple, weighing and unloading the coal as it was brought up from the tunnels. Two of the Inman girls were about the same age as Frances and Vera. Frances and Vera would sometimes spend the night with Edna and Hannah. What's two more in an already crowded bed? Edna and Hannah would also spend the night at the Elliott's house. The two families were related, however, it was a complicated kinship. It involved Great-Grandpa Meyers having children with two wives and having additional children with the second wife. He outlived both wives. The Elliott clan was also related to Oscar and Kate Meyers and John and Mary McDonald, all who lived on the ridge. Most other families living on the ridge had relatives living there as well.

Shorty Inman owned a sugar cane processing business where he processed sugar cane into molasses. Many farmers would raise the sugar cane and then bring it to Shorty for processing into molasses. In the late fall, the sugar cane would be ready to harvest. The first step was for all the children to take a wooden stick and beat the foliage off the standing sugar cane. Then the older boys would hitch the mule to the wagon, and with a long machete type of knife, they would cut the bare sugar cane stalks off right at the ground and stack them lengthwise on the wagon. The wagon load of sugar cane was then taken to the Inmans for processing. The sugar cane was unloaded up next to the crushing machine which crushed the cane to squeeze the juice from the cane. The crushing machine consisted of two sets of rollers. As the rollers turned, a worker had to feed the sugar cane into the turning rollers. The crushed cane stalks then exited the rollers and the clear juice was collected in a large tub beneath the rollers. The crushing mill had a U-shaped steel shaft extending above the top of the mill. This shaft was attached to the roller below through a series of gears. A long pole about twenty-five feet long was bolted to the U-shaped portion of the shaft. At the extreme end of the twenty-five-foot pole, a horse or mule was hitched. The mule proceeded to go round and round in a twenty-five feet circle, providing the power to turn the rollers which crushed the cane. A pipe fitted into the catching tub transferred the raw juice downhill to the cooking vat. The vat was made of solid copper and was about one foot deep, four feet wide, and twelve feet long. The cooking vat had four baffle plates equally spaced along the length of the vat. The vat was raised up above the ground about eighteen inches so a fire could be maintained under the vat during the cooking process. As the greenish colored raw juice drained into the cooking vat, the cook would slowly work it through the four baffled sections. Using his eyes and nose, Shorty would use a wooden paddle to move the juice through all the baffles until it turned a golden amber color and thickened to the right consistency. At the end of the cooking, a valve would be opened and the molasses drained into empty one gallon tin cans. Lids were then used to seal the gallon tins of molasses. Shorty would usually receive about one fourth of the syrup as his portion for doing the cooking and the remainder went to the one who supplied the cane. Most grocery stores were very eager to get the syrup. It was in high demand by the city folks and usually sold for about three dollars per gallon. The quality of the syrup varied from year to year. If the weather was too dry and hot, the syrup would be very dark and strong flavored. If there was ample rain and moderate temperatures, the syrup would be a golden amber color and very sweet and mild.

Great-Grandpa Meyers lived with the Inmans. I suspect he was the original owner of the log cabin and perhaps built the home himself. Originally, much of the deeded land on the ridge belonged to great Grandpa Meyers. Later, during the depression and when he had gotten older, he sold off most of his land. By the midthirties, Great-Grandpa Meyers was a very old man. He had a long white beard and walked with difficulty. The Inmans built a small room on the end of the house which was attached to the house by a breeze-way. This is where Great-Grandpa Meyers lived. This room had a stairway which led up to a small attic room above his room. As children, we were always curious about what was in that attic room. We liked to play on the stairway, but Great-Grandpa Meyers watched the stairs like a hawk. Whenever we got too far up those steps, he would yell, "Git outna thar!" None of us kids ever found out what was in that attic room. Some speculated that was where he stashed his moonshine.

About one-fourth mile west of the Inman home was a small frame home where fiddling Al Wilson lived. Al was an older man, and he and his wife did not have any children still living with them. Al was known for his pedigree walker fox hounds. He loved to fox hunt and was out in the woods three or four times a week running his dogs. If he wasn't out with his fox hounds, he was most likely sitting on the front porch playing his fiddle. Sometimes others would join him and there would be a regular bluegrass jamboree which could go on for hours.

A short distance further west from fiddling Al's house was Ma Files's house. It was one of the larger homes on the ridge. It had a porch extending all the way across the front of the house and also extended across the east side. Ma Files lived alone most of the time, but sometimes relatives would come and stay with her for long periods of time. During the depression years, a relative, Ted Swindle, and his teenage daughters lived with Ma Files. The two girls had a reputation for being wild. I was too young to know much about that, but I do know they could cuss up a blue streak! Ma Files had lost her husband sometime before the mid-1930s. Most widowed women had to resort to living with a daughter or son if her husband died. Somehow Ma Files was able to maintain her home, perhaps because she was healthy or perhaps because one of her sons lived only a few hundred feet west of her house.

Edger Files's wife and daughter died sometime in the early 1940s. They both contracted tuberculosis. After his wife and daughter died, Edger was left with three young sons, Jerry, Billy, and Kip. Ma Files cooked and cared for these three boys while Edger was away at work. She assigned them chores to do each day. She was a grouchy talking woman who dipped snuff. She always had a tin can container of snuff in her apron pocket. The snuff was placed behind the lower lip in front of the lower front teeth. It required a constant spitting to rid the mouth of the excessive tobacco juice. Usually an empty tin can was always within spitting distance. Outside, however, the juice was simply spat upon the ground. Ma Files was constantly grumbling and fussing at the children. Once she stated that if there was any work needing to be done, then Jerry had to go to the outhouse. Except she was more graphic than that! She said, "Anytime there's work to be done, Jerry has got to go sh**."

All the children seemed to annoy her, but to the children, it appeared to be a case of all bark and no bite. She was liked by the children and her front yard was one of their favorite places to play. Out in the front yard was a very large white oak tree. It was probably three hundred years old and about five feet in diameter at the trunk. There was always a swing hanging from one of its massive limbs. The ground under the tree was packed hard and void of any vegetation. It was maintained firm and smooth for the boy's marble games. Almost every boy from six to fifteen carried around a bag of marbles. The objective of playing marbles wasn't about simply playing marbles but rather about how many marbles you could win by playing keeps. Each boy would place an equal number of marbles in the very center of a large diameter circle drawn in the dirt. The circle was about five or six feet in diameter. If there were five boys playing, then each would place five marbles in the center for a total of twenty-five marbles tightly bunched in the center. The order for shooting would be determined by tossing your shooter marble toward a line drawn in the dirt about twelve feet away. The closest to the line you got without going over it would determine who got to shoot first. Then all the other turns would be determined by your proximity to the line. The game would began with the first shooter placing his knuckles right on the line of the large circle. With the shooter resting between his thumb and index finger, the thumb was used to propel the shooter marble toward the cluster of marbles in the middle of the circle. A good powerful impact of the shooter into the cluster of marbles would send them flying in every direction. If any of the marbles were knocked out of the large circle and your shooter remained inside the circle, then you could continue to shoot until you either failed to knock a marble outside the circle or else you missed and your shooter left the circle. Then it would be the next boy's turn. Each boy kept all the marbles he knocked outside the circle until there were none left in the circle. Then a new game would start. Usually the game ended when most of the boys had lost their marbles to the most accurate shooters. Vora considered this a form of gambling and didn't like it when we played for keeps. Sometimes the whole Sunday afternoon would be spent playing marbles.

From Ma Files's house continuing west about three hundred yards was Edger Files's house. Edger's house was right at the place where the road coming up the hill intersected with the east to west road. His house place provided a spectacular view of the entire small town down in the valley. The children would often look out over the valley and try to locate the school building, the post office, or a friend's house. It was quite difficult to do from that distance; all the buildings seemed to be meshed together, so it was difficult to locate individual places. It was always exciting to be in that location when a train came speeding through the small town. The children would all count the number of railroad cars being pulled by the engine. In the late 1940s, the small town erected a huge five-pointed star in front of Edger's house. During the Christmas holidays, the star would shine every night. Strands of electric lights would form the outline of the five points on the star. Up close on the ridge, it was an ugly, gaudy construction of old utility poles with two by four framing, but from the small town, everyone thought it was beautiful.

I don't recall which died first, Edger's wife or daughter, but I think it was the daughter. The beautiful young teenage daughter was brought home from the hospital and placed in an iron lung in the sitting room of the Files's home. She was in this contraption almost all time. It made very weird noises and the younger children didn't like to be around it. Vora visited the Files family shortly after the daughter was brought home. She carried the twins with her on the visit. Soon after the visit, the young girl died. It wasn't very long afterward that everyone on the ridge received a notice from the County Health Department informing them that they were required to get a chest x-ray. A mobile x-ray unit arrived, and everyone received a schedule as to when they would get their x-ray. Vora assured us that it wouldn't hurt, and it was just a precautionary measure. Some of the younger children were very worried and were afraid they might have tuberculosis. Within two weeks, the results came back through the mail. How frightful it was when both Vora and Louis were informed they must come back to the County Health Department for another x-ray! They complied with the order and had more x-rays taken. No further communication was ever received from the Health Department.

In the mid-1930s, during the Great Depression, Great-Grandpa Meyers decided to sell most of his land. He approached Jonny first about purchasing the bottom land, which consisted of about 240 acres. The asking price was about six thousand dollars. Jonny really wanted to buy the land, but money was scarce, and he would have had to borrow the money to make the purchase. Vora felt they just shouldn't go that deeply in debt and shouldn't buy the land. The land was then sold to Edger Files. In about 1945, a coal company contracted with Edger to strip mine the bottom land and extract the coal. Edger received a great deal of money from the sale of this coal. Jonny always grieved about his failure to purchase the land. When Vora would complain about not having enough money to pay the bills, Jonny would remind her of how she prevented him from purchasing the land and making a fortune from the sale of the coal.

Only about one hundred feet away from Edger's house was the Castleberry house. It was a neat house but very small. The Castleberrys had only one child, Fay. Mr. Castleberry was a well-educated man and worked either for the state or federal government as an auditor. He was a large, heavyset man with very thick glasses. He would usually leave home on Monday mornings and not return until the weekend. The older teenage boys would gossip about how Edger would often go over to the Castleberry's house and do some maintenance chores for Mrs. Cassleberry when Mr. Cassleberry was away. They would say, "Sometimes it takes Edger three hours to replace a burnt out lamp bulb for Mrs. Castleberry!"

Continuing on down the road about half a mile was another of the log-style homes. About one half of the log home had rotten away and the roof had fallen in. The yard around the home was overgrown with thick brush and vines. The log home had the typical breezeway and the bedroom section had totally collapsed due to neglect. *The home was still occupied!* Monroe Stovall still lived alone in the remaining part which was still standing. Only a small well-worn pathway leading to the door provided a clue that someone was living there. Monroe was a happy-go-lucky man who worked for a while at the town post office. Sometimes he would work, other times he would just hang out at the town pool hall. When he would walk back home to his rundown shack, he would always be whistling. The ridge children made up a song about Monroe which they sang to the tune of "Jingle Bells."

Mon-er-row, Mon-er-row,
Whistling ore the hills.

There weren't many verses, but it was sang over and over when they heard Monroe coming up the road whistling. Monroe had adult children who had moved away but apparently lost his wife very early in life. Many of the ridge people had lost their mates early in life. Perhaps with the loss of a loving mate, Monroe had simply lost interest in his empty home and just let it rot away. It was a great mystery to the children how Monroe could be so happy and at the same time live in such squalor. Monroe's house was situated on approximately two hundred acres of land. The land showed evidence of once being farmed, but most of it was now overgrown like the house place. He always kept a flock of chickens which roamed all over the hills by day but came back to the fallen down portion of the house to roost at night. Monroe just seemed to ignore the chickens as well.

Continuing around a curve about one-fourth mile west of Monroe's shack was a home occupied by a single woman about Vora's age. Dellah Whitley had an adult daughter but was never married. None of the ridge wives ever talked about the out-of-wedlock child. The adult daughter often visited Dellah and was an attractive young woman. She was the first woman I ever saw who smoked cigarettes openly and publically. Dellah was a rather plump woman with large bosoms. She was very jovial and loved children. When Vora would walk by Dellah's house on the way to visit the Inmans, Dellah would always run out to greet Vora and the twins. She was particularly fond of Louis. Dellah would sweep Louis up in her arms and squeeze him tightly, burying his face in those large sweaty bosoms! She would exclaim, "That's the purtest child I've ever seen!" Dellah rented about twenty acres of land directly in front of her house from Monroe. She had the land cleared, and year after year would plant it with corn. This was a mystery to the younger children because Dellah had no horses, cattle, or chickens. What did she do with all that corn? Later we understood; Dellah was a bootlegger. She sold moonshine whiskey which was illegal since Walker County was supposed to be a dry county. However, it wasn't difficult to find booze in Walker County. Dellah's brother lived deep in the forest around Wolf Creek and was purported to have a whiskey still where he used Dellah's corn crop to make the moonshine. Dellah provided the whiskey to the coal miners and many of the upstanding business owners who lived in the small town. Even the off-duty policemen would occasionally be spied frequenting Dellah's house!

The next two houses just west of Dellah's house are clustered very close together as compared to most of the other homes. The road makes a sharp turn to the west as it continues almost due west. Just at the curve was the Adkins home. A single lane road extends due east about two hundred feet back to the Childers home. The Childers home was a very neat but small home. It was painted white. Lois Childers was an elementary school teacher and her deceased husband had also been a school teacher. They had only two children, a boy called Sonny and a younger daughter called Sissy. Also living with them were the children's grandmother and great-grandmother. Sonny and Sissy were not allowed to play with the other ridge children very often. The only way Sonny could play with the other ridge children was if he could slip away from his grandmothers. They would tell him, "You're too smart to play with those children." Due to Sonny's mother and father both being college educated, they wanted Sonny and Sissy to identify with and play with the more refined city children. They were above associating with the ridge children. This was very unfortunate because Sonny loved to play with us when he could and always had great fun on the bus as he rode to and from school. Sadly, both

Sonny and Sissy generally ended up being confined to their own yards and isolated from the other ridge children. Sonny never married. He graduated from college and returned to teach in the small town's high school as a science teacher. Sissy got married shortly after high school, but her marriage didn't work out and she was soon divorced. She ended up with some serious mental health issues and lived an unhappy life. Sonny taught at the high school until retirement and died soon after retirement.

The Adkins family had four boys and no girls. The father, Oscar Atkins, was a coal miner. Delmar was his wife. They had two older boys named Luke and Dick. The two older boys moved away to Chicago when the coal mines began closing. Prior to moving to Chicago, Luke worked at the Galloway Coal Mine Company store as a butcher. They both worked in Chicago as city bus drivers. Then Dick got a job driving a Greyhound bus. He had a uniform, got to drive a bus, and made a lot of money! That's what the two younger boys, Bobby and Joe, boasted about. At the time, I dreamed about one day having a job driving a big Greyhound bus! The family visited Chicago once, and Joe described in detail how big Chicago was and how bitterly cold it was in the winter. I listened intently to Joe's description of Chicago. To me it was like some very far away foreign country, which I probably would never see. Bobby Ray was about Fred's age and Joe (everyone called Jody) was about one year younger than me. Jody and I played together a great deal. Jody was a wimpy child and didn't enjoy any type of contact sports. When Jody was about six years old, his father was injured very severely in a mining accident. There was a cave-in and his back was broken, and he was paralyzed from his waist down. He was sent home from the hospital after the accident and was confined to a bed in the sitting room. Oscar never recovered and died about six months after the accident. Bobby Ray had graduated from school and joined the army. The only ones left home were Delmar and Jody. About two years after Oscar's death, tragedy struck again. One early morning, the Atkins home burned down. With nowhere to live, Luke came back from Chicago, and Delmar and Jody packed up what few belongings which had been salvaged from the fire. They moved to Chicago and I never saw Jody again.

The next home, about one-fourth mile westward, was the Elliott house. It sat back from the main road about one hundred yards and the lane circled the house and again intersected with the main road about one hundred yards west of the house. This lane was the walking pathway of all the neighbors from both the eastern and western ends of the plateau as they took the pathway through the pasture toward town. This pathway was a shortcut, saving a lot of walking distance as opposed to walking the roads. The Elliott homestead contained forty acres of land, about half of which could be farmed and the remainder a steep heavily wooded hillside. The Elliott family, Jonny, Vora, and six of the seven children have already been described and further discussion will be withheld until later.

About half a mile on westward was the home of Kate and Oscar Meyers. Their house was fairly small. They had about ten acres of land, none of which was cultivated. Oscar Meyers was related somehow to Jonny through the lineage of Great-Grandpa Meyers. The Meyers children were similar in age to the older Elliott children. The oldest, Dugan, was the same age as James Elliott. There was a daughter about Frances's age and another boy Vera's age. James and Dugan were good buddies and finished high school together. Being buddies, they enlisted in the army at the beginning of World War II. They both went to Europe to fight Nazi Germany.

James came back in the late spring of 1945, but Dugan didn't make it back until about 1950. I attended his closed casket funeral, but James didn't attend. He never explained why, but perhaps memories of Dugan were best preserved in fond memories of their good times as teenagers roaming the hills and exploring the wonders of nature. Sadly, Dugan's young life was one of thousands cut short by a tragic death on the battlefields somewhere in Europe. Typically of many young ridge children, Kathrine Meyers moved to Birmingham shortly after graduating from high school. The youngest son, Bob, like Dugan, was an outstanding football player. He was offered a scholarship to play football for Auburn University. He went to Auburn for about two weeks before returning home. Auburn was just too far away from home. Later he moved to Birmingham and got a job in the steel mills. He would often stop by James's house for a visit as they lived very close to one another. Oscar was a coal miner and walked down the lane by the Elliott's house daily going to and from work. Sometimes, on payday, he wouldn't make it home in the evenings. Oftentimes he could be found sleeping off a hangover at the bottom of the hill beside the pathway leading to town. He and several other men could frequently be found sleeping off a drinking binge. As the children would walk by these sleeping men, they were very quiet so they wouldn't awaken them. Kate was a warm friendly lady. She was very much a homebody and didn't visit others very often. She did however enjoy having others visit her. No telephones existed on the ridge. Porch sitting was a very important means of communication.

Beyond the Meyer's house a narrow road turned abruptly to the southeast and extended deep into the woods. It was so narrow that wagons or vehicles could not pass each other without finding a place suitable for pulling off the road.

Otherwise, it would be very difficult to back a vehicle on the narrow road. This didn't pose a significant problem; rarely did anyone in a vehicle meet another on that road. About a mile down this narrow lane was the Hendrix home. Dewey and his wife Sadie and their six children lived in this house. There was about twenty acres on this homestead. Most of it was in pasture where they kept a milk cow. They did own a mule at one time, but it died in the small stable one night. Since it could not be dragged out through the narrow doorway to the stable, John Delevicheo brought his team of mules up to the Hendrix house and tied a rope around the dead mule's hind legs. Then his team of mules pulled the dead mule through the doorway, breaking bones and squeezing the carcass through the doorway! The Hendrix house was built up off the ground about two feet. This afforded a fun place to play on rainy days. None of the homes had basements, and they were all built well above the ground. Most likely this was designed to ward off termite and carpenter ants invasions.

Underneath the house in the dry sand were little critters the children called doodle bugs. These strange-looking little creatures were about the size of a house fly but with no wings. They would build small craters in the loose dirt and then hide inside the walls, waiting for a carpenter ant or other small bug to fall into the crater. Then they would spring out from their hiding place and devour their victim. The children would take a chicken feather or small twig and gently touch the inside of the crater. When the doodle bug sprang out, they would catch them. It was like hunting; each child competed with the others to see who could catch the most doodle bugs. Underneath every house would be colonies of doodle bugs. The Hendrix children ranged in age span similar to the Elliott clan. The two older boys were in the military service during the war and made a career out of their service in the navy. There was a daughter about Frances's age who moved to Birmingham after finishing high school. Another daughter was about Fred's age. Fred got much teasing about Doris being his girlfriend by John Jr. and James. Another son, Frank, was about a year younger than the twins, and another son, Terry, was two years younger than Frank. Frank, who was always called Frankie, was a close playmate of Louis. When playing over at the Hendrix house with Frankie, Terry would always want to play with us. Frankie disliked Terry always wanting to hang out with him and his friends. There was much fussing between these brothers. Sometimes it would escalate into a good pounding by Frankie. Terry was very stubborn and tough. Frankie couldn't discourage Terry to leave us alone. Terry became an outstanding football player at the small town's high school.

Continuing on beyond the Hendrix home on this narrow road for about another mile was the Delevechio homestead. The bachelor, Jim Delevechio, lived in another of the log-cabin-style homes. It appeared very old and, like Monroe Stovall's home, one half of the home had been allowed to rot away. Jim owned about three hundred acres of land, much of it in a very flat fertile valley with a small stream running through it. Jim had nailed up No Trespassing signs all around his property lines. Jim was not a recluse. He was friendly when he came by on his way to town. However, he preferred that no one come on his property unless they had good reason to do so. Jim had a nice log-style barn and a pair of beautiful light-brown mules almost identical in size and color. I don't think anyone could tell which mule was which except Jim. He also had a beautiful two-horse wagon which I admired very much. It was painted green with red trim. The seat at the front of the wagon was mounted on springs, so it provided a comfortable ride on the rough roads. Sometimes when the children caught Jim coming back up the hill with his wagon, they would hitch a ride on the back of the wagon. I understand Jim was wounded in World War I and received a government disability check each month. He also used his fine team of mules to mow hay fields for other farmers. He owned a mowing machine and rake that was pulled by the mules. He also raised a substantial amount of corn each year. There was a small cemetery near the front yard of Jim's house. There were three grave markers in this cemetery. Two of the graves were adults, and there was also one which appeared to be a small child. No names were on the markers. Sometimes there were rumors about Jim having buried treasure on his property. That's why he had all the No Trespassing signs. I never felt this to be nothing but silly rumors. However, several years later, a group of thugs attacked Jim on his property demanding that Jim give them the location of his treasure. Jim almost died from this attack. I don't know if he managed to make it up to the Hendrix home to get help or just how he was discovered, but he was taken to the hospital in Birmingham. He was in the hospital for several weeks. Since James Elliott now lived in Birmingham, he often visited with Jim during his recovery. On numerous occasions during the depression, Jonny often borrowed money from Jim to pay off some debts. Jonny always managed to pay it back. Jonny and Jim were good friends. The Elliott boys were often hired by Jim to help weed the corn. The going rate was three dollars per day for about twelve hours. We never looked at the clock. When it began to get dark, then the work stopped. The boys were very glad to get the opportunity to work and earn some money. They would bring their earnings to Vora for the family expenses. She would always give them something back, usually two quarters. She would tell them to buy something they wanted. It was usually spent on ice cream down at the store. A single scoop of ice cream in a cone was five cents. By being careful, this could supply treats for about a month. Usually, however, treats were often bought for a brother or sister or a friend, and the money was gone within a single visit to the store.

Just a short distance west from where the small lane turned off to go to the Hendrix and Delevichio homes was where the McDonald and Ma Elliott home was located. This house was located just at the point where the road curved northward and descended back down No. 11 Hill to the valley below. Ma Elliott's husband had passed away many years ago, and Ma Elliott would live for a while with one daughter and then another. I believe the McDonald home was originally one which belonged to Ma Elliott and her deceased husband. There was about eighty acres of land with this home. This home was partially log style and partially wood siding. It had been altered sometime in the past. The sitting room and kitchen were also separated from the bedrooms by the typical dog run. Mary McDonald was Jonny's sister. The McDonalds had seven children which almost paralleled the Elliott children age wise. The oldest girl was about the same age as John Jr., and there was another girl Vera's age. Another daughter, Margret, was Fred's age and then there was a daughter, Alma, the same age as Lois and Louis. There were two children, a boy and a girl, younger than Lois and Louis. The boy, Henry, was about two year younger than the twins, and the youngest daughter was about ten years younger than the twins. Alma and the twins often played together, and Louis also played quite a bit with Henry. John McDonald was an avid hunter and very successful at it. He always had a pack of blue tick hounds he used for raccoon hunting at night. John hunted several nights a week and seemed to maintain his orientation through the vast woodland even at night. He would often kill three or four raccoons per night. Raccoon fur or pelts were in great demand for making fur coats. A nice raccoon pelt could bring twenty-five dollars. The raccoons would be very carefully skinned with a razor sharp knife in order to get all the meat off the skin. Then the pelt would be turned inside out and stretched over a board for drying. The board with the raccoon pelt would be nailed high upon the side of the barn so no critters could get to it. They would hang there until the skin was completely dry. Then several would be taken down and packed into a box to be shipped to the processing plant. John worked some in the coal mines but never really worked full time in the mine. He probably made more off the raccoon pelts than he made as a miner. In the early 1950s, John moved with his family to California. The three youngest children moved to California with their parents; some of the older children also moved there later. When John retired from his job in California, he and all the children moved back to Alabama. John built a new house on the ridge within a few hundred feet from their old home place. By then, the old home place had either burned or was torn down. The land had been converted into a cattle ranch.

At the point where the main road turned northward and began its descent down No. 11 Hill, another very narrow one-lane road continued westward approximately one and a half miles into the woods. It was very similar to the road to the Hendrix and Delevichio homes. At the end of this lane was another log home in which the Swindles lived. This was also of the log-cabin-style homes with the typical dog run separating the bedrooms from the sitting room and kitchen. Bervel Swindle and his wife and six children lived in this home. They lived so far back in the woods that the children didn't go over there to play very often. I can't remember the name of Bervel's wife. This family was very poor. And all the family were sickly. A young son, James Paul, was close in age to Louis. He was in poor health and seldom came out to play. Their mother was also sickly and seemed to suffer from dementia or some other malady. The whole family lived in deep poverty. Bervel was a self-employed carpenter, and during the depression era, there was little work for a carpenter. I always admired his woodworking skills. He made the handles for all his woodworking and farming tools. All his handmade handles and tools looked store bought!

Once, James Paul became very ill. His body became swollen all over and he lay in a coma for several days. I don't believe he received any type of medical attention. Being so poor and so isolated back in the woods, families often resorted to home remedies and prayer to pull them through. James Paul eventually recovered, but he did not return to school for months. No one ever understood what had caused this illness. The Swindles had a big black and white dog they named Eisenhower. He was a great squirrel dog. As teenagers, we usually would go over to the Swindles to borrow Eisenhower. in the afternoon when we got home from school to go squirrel hunting.

As the road twisted and turned steeply down No. 11 Hill to the valley below, there was a group of former mining camp houses called Bynum Camp located at the bottom of the hill. There were children who lived in these houses that were friends of the ridge children as well. The Thornbros, Estells, Wilkersons, and Bynums were just a few of the approximately twenty families living in Bynum Camp. They became friends as they all were on the same bus going to and from school.

Sometime in the early 1950s, an accountant was moved to the small town to handle the final closing of the Galloway Coal Mining Company's business. His name was

Mr. Morrow. Mr. Morrow was a devoted Christian man and almost like a pied piper when it came to his association with children. He loved children and was a member of the small town's Church of Christ located on the north end of town. He began teaching the children's Bible classes and was so enthusiastic that he soon filled the church building with children. Soon the church bought a used school bus which made runs up to the ridge people, Bynum Camp, and then north of the small town to a place called Dog Town. When the bus arrived back to the small church, it would be filled to capacity with children. It was great fun on the bus even though it would occasionally break down and leave the children stranded until the town mechanic would arrive to get it going again. Unfortunately, after approximately two years, Mr. Morrow was relocated elsewhere and much of the energy' and enthusiasm he had created faded away, just like the small town continued to fade away.

Sequel (Circa 1936 — 1941): The Ridge Folks

It's dinnertime in the small town. A merchant, owner of the general merchandise store located on the main street of the small town, locks his store and walks up the hill toward his nice home. His evening meal awaits him. He sits down to a great meal of roast beef, mashed potatoes, and vegetables his wife has prepared. The house is comfortable. It's heated by a new automatic furnace just installed. He's still dressed in his white business shirt and tie. After the fine meal, the paunchy little man retires to the sitting parlor. He slightly adjusts the thermostat controlling the newly installed coker coal furnace. He then lights a cigar and sits down to read his evening paper. His wife brings him a glass of wine from their newly acquired electric refrigerator. He relaxes. He thinks, "Life is good. It doesn't get any better than this!"

Approximately three miles due south, deep in the forest, Jim Delvicheo rises from his comfortable chair on his porch. He has been there for over two hours, gazing out over the beautiful valley. It's suppertime. He enters the portion of the house still intact and begins to build a fire in the kitchen stove. He lights a kerosene lamp to provide light while he cooks his meal. He's already cleaned and cut up the squirrel he killed a few hours ago. While the fire begins to heat up the stove, he takes the water bucket out in his front yard to fetch some fresh water from the well to brew his evening coffee. When he returns into the house, the fire is now ready to cook his meal. He fries the squirrel meat in pork fat using a large cast-iron frying pan. He simmers some fresh polk greens he gathered early in the morning around the barn. Once the squirrel is a golden brown and the polk greens are tender, he sits down with his coffee, corn bread, fried squirrel, and polk greens. It's so tasty! Jim thinks, "Life is good. It doesn't get any better than this!"

It's transition time in the Appalachian mountains! Only a remnant of the ridge people still live like Jim. He still has his mules and fancy wagon. He still enjoys sitting on his porch and looking out over the beautiful valley. The fertile soil causes the pasture grass to take on a deep green color. He can see the sunlight shimmering off the water in the gently flowing small stream along the base of the mountain. The mountains are filled with virgin hardwood timber. Stately oak, hickory, beech, maple, and pine trees all remain standing, undisturbed in their places on the side of the hill.

Jim finishes his meal. His eye catches the old shoe box up in the cupboard above the stove. It contains some cash and two government retirement checks. The checks remind him that he needs to go to town soon and deposit the checks in his already substantial savings account. The depression years had not harmed Jim.

Fast forward 60 years...

Jim is dead. So is the paunchy little merchant. Jim lies in the small family cemetery which provides a spectacular view of the beautiful valley, the small stream, and the virgin forest. It's a peaceful place, a restful place. The four graves are marked with stones carefully selected from the bank of the small stream. The paunchy little merchant lies in a prominent site in the small town cemetery. His grave is marked with an impressive marble headstone. Its engraved lettering identifies who is buried there, when he was born, and when he died, nothing more. When Jim died, his estate was willed to a lone survivor, a nephew. Soon after Jim's death the nephew sold off the timber. The hills were stripped of all the stately trees. The nephew received several hundred thousand dollars for the timber. He bought a fine new home; a new Cadillac automobile, and even his own private airplane! That wasn't enough! Next he sold the mineral rights to a coal company to strip mine the coal. The large bulldozers and shovels moved into the peaceful little valley. They stripped away the fine fertile soil from the valley. They diverted the natural course of the small stream. They raped the entire little valley to extract her precious black gold that had been there since God placed it there. They left the small family cemetery intact. It sits on about a city block of land which was spared from the ravage destruction of the bulldozers and shovels. Why save it? Surely Jim, his pioneer mother and father, and their infant daughter must now hate the view! Besides, a substantial amount of coal still remains under that cemetery plot (maybe one hundred thousand dollars or more.) When will they go after that as well?

In about 1950, John McDonald moved his family to Southern California seeking work. He remained there approximately twenty-five years. Upon retiring, John returned to the ridge and built a retirement home. Soon afterward, Dick and Luke Atkins returned back to the ridge. They built two fine brick homes, one on the very site where Delma's home had burned many years earlier. When Fred Elliott retired from the Redstone Arsenal in Huntsville, Alabama, he returned to live in the old Elliott homestead. He made some improvements to it, and it still remains in possession of Fred. His son currently lives there. Why? Did some mystical power within their DNA genomic material lure them back? What causes some to be happy and content without the fluff and others who can only be happy if they have it? I myself still feel this sense of belonging when I return to the hills. After sixty years away, there's still that mysterious allure in the hills which whispers, "Welcome home." It causes one to wonder, what is the motivation? The hills are still there but much has changed in and around them. Anger wells up within my being when I see the destruction created by the strip mines. Someday a scientific analysis of your gnome ribbons may determine where you would be best suited to live. What location on this good earth would be most suitable for you? Might that not be the root source of discontentment in the world today? Maybe our gnome ribbons are telling us to go home!

In my letters so far, I've tried to paint a scene of picturesque hills covered with stately trees, peaceful valleys rich with mineral deposits, and crystal clear flowing streams. A picture of small towns springing up in the mid-1800s due to the coal mines. Thriving then struggling and dying as the natural resources are exhausted. Ridge people who were attached to the land almost as closely and as spiritually as the Native American Indians. A picture of dark and sad times when small towns and cities alike struggled with racism, social and economic injustices, and a time of transition from rural to urban living. A time when fathers struggled to support their children and mothers struggling to stretch the family budget in order to feed and clothe their children. A time when families of all race and creeds reached across all social-economic barriers, united in a just cause to sacrifice their young boys in a struggle against fascism. A transition time when the shrill, lonesome whistle of the steam engine locomotive gave way to the powerful and resonate sounds of the diesel locomotives roaring through the small town, not needing to stop anymore to take on more coal or water.

But now, by far, the most difficult challenge is before me—to write my personal story of a child from day one until nineteen years old. My many memories, most good, some not so good. My abiding love and appreciation of family, of friends, land and forest, hills and amazing night skies, and plain, simple people who helped mold me into who I am today; who, just like the hills and valleys, will always be a part of me no matter where I live or how long I live!

Have a great week, grandson. Much love from your favorite grandpa.

The Seventh Child: Louis
First to Fifth Years

It was May 13, 1936. Breakfast seemed normal that morning to the five children. John Jr. and James had gotten their instructions on what they should do today at the evening meal the night before. John Jr. was instructed to take a mule and the garden cultivator up to Ma Elliott's house and cultivate her sizeable garden and potato patch. The McDonald children would then take their hoes and finish cleaning the garden and potato patch of all weeds. James was to begin plowing the ten-acre cornfield just south of the house. James selected ole Frank as his mule to plow the cornfield. Frank moved faster than ole Beck and James's temperament was better suited for a faster pace. John Jr. had to hitch ole Beck to the wagon and load the garden cultivator into the wagon. Normally if you only needed the turning plow, you could just hitch the mule directly to the turning plow, then lay the plow on its side and let it drag along the road to the work site. The cultivator could not be dragged, however, because the cultivator's plows were spring mounted and might snag on a rock and break. By the time John Jr. had loaded the wagon and started up the lane toward the McDonalds, James had already made several passes through the cornfield. He was using an eight-inch plow sweep which would require two passes in each of the corn row middles. The purpose was to clean the weeds and grass from between the rows of corn. It required a great deal of concentration and alertness. If the plow got too close to the corn, it might rip the corn out by its roots or perhaps cover the corn up by the freshly turned dirt.

It was a bright sunny day and James knew that by noon it would be hot. He was eager to get as much plowing done as he could while there was a gentle morning breeze. As he turned the mule around at the east end of the cornfield, he noticed Frances running up the lane going toward the McDonald house. James thought, "She's already finished washing the breakfast dishes and swept the floor and now mother is letting her go up to the McDonalds to play with Louise and Virginia." He continued to plow. Plowing is a good time for thinking. It was good now to be out of school for the summer. Soon the water in the creek would be warm enough to go for a swim after plowing all day. In about another week, the wild plums would be ready for eating. They were very sweet and full of juice. Noticing their rich red color, James reckoned they would be ready for picking in about a week. He would have to watch carefully or else the blue jays and robins would beat him to the plums. There was a sweet fragrance in the cool morning breeze from all the wild honeysuckle vines and fruit trees in bloom.

As he turned ole Frank at the end of the cornfield, he noticed Frances and Ma Elliott walking very fast, as fast as an old woman crippled with arthritis could walk. James thought, "I wonder why Ma Elliott is coming for a visit so early?" Then he remembered, "It's almost time for the new baby to be born. I wonder if that's why Frances went to fetch Ma Elliott?" He continued to plow. He knew it wasn't anything he'd be allowed to do inside the house anyway. Usually, the older children would be sent off to a neighbor's house while a baby was being delivered. He'd know in due time; meanwhile, there's plowing needing to be done. It wasn't a happy occasion anyway. It was a bad time to be having children. The Great Depression had settled in very hard all over the entire country. Vora was unhappy about becoming pregnant. Her mother, Ma Rosie, had scolded her and made statements like, "That's just what you need, another mouth to feed."

Ma Elliott entered the house breathing very hard due to hastily walking that mile with Frances. She noticed the fire in the kitchen stove was still hot from cooking the breakfast meal. She told Vera to put a pot of water on the stove to warm. Ma Elliott and Frances went into the bedroom where Vora was sitting on the edge of the bed. She was in obvious pain. Ma Elliott told Frances to wait outside the door in the sitting room and to listen in case she called for her. Ma Elliott tried to remember all the babies she had helped deliver. There had been many, and she was confident this would be just another routine delivery. If everything went as expected, she would be back home in three or four hours.

Frances and Vera stood just outside the doorway, listening intently as they anticipated hearing the unmistakable cry of a new born baby. Vera was distracted by Fred as he wandered into the room. In her excitement, Vera had forgotten about Fred. She helped him put on his bib overalls with the suspenders crossed behind his back. Ma Elliott called for Vera to check the water on the stove to see if it was warm. Vera ran into the kitchen and dipped her finger in the water. It was warm. She ran back into the sitting room and called through the closed door to Ma Elliott, letting her know the water was warm. Ma Elliott told her to pour some water into the wash pan and to bring it with some clean towels quickly. Ma Elliott opened the door slightly and took the water and towels into the bedroom. Everything seemed under control. Ma Elliott didn't think it would be necessary to send James into town to tell Dr. Manasco to come over. Vera and Frances stood outside in the sitting room. They could hear the deep rapid breathing of their mother. She occasionally moaned as in deep pain.

After what seemed to be an endless wait, they heard the unmistakable cry of a baby. They looked at one another and broke out in big smiles. They were very anxious to come into the room and see the new baby! Ma Elliott quickly washed the new baby and wrapped it in a blanket. She then turned her attention to Vora to try to make her comfortable and tell her she had another beautiful baby girl. As she looked at Vora, she knew something wasn't right. She quickly detected the head of another baby emerging. It's the first time, she thought, that she had ever delivered a multiple birth. The second baby was gently pulled from the birth canal and now Ma Elliott had her hands full. She washed the boy baby and then called for Frances to come in and assist her.

Ma Elliott noticed the baby boy was in distress. It appeared he wasn't breathing and his color was ashen. Ma Elliott began to massage the small infant's body. She stretched his arms over his head and she gently compressed his chest. He still didn't appear to be breathing. Ma Elliott then placed her mouth over the infant's nose and mouth and blew her breath into the infant's lungs. She watched to make sure the infant's chest expanded with her breath. She worked very hard and aggressively on the baby. She didn't want this baby to die! She continued to work diligently on the baby for several hours. She pumped his arms up and down, she breathed into his nose and mouth, and was somewhat relieved as the infant began to breathe on his own.

Vora watched intently and in total shock. She had no idea she was pregnant with twins. Two babies! Two more babies! Seven children! Times are bad and now there's two more mouths to feed! Ma Elliott told Frances to run out where James was plowing and tell him to run as fast as he could over to Dr. Manasco's house and tell him to come quickly because there was a very sick newborn baby. Frances told James, "Mother had a baby girl and a baby boy!"

James quickly tied ole Frank to a small tree at the end of the corn rows. He left the rein long enough so the mule could graze on the grass along the fence row. Barefooted and shirtless, James ran as fast as he could over to Dr. Manasco's house. His office was in the front parlor of his large stately house. Within ten minutes, James was knocking on the doctor's parlor door. Dr. Manasco's wife answered the door. James exclaimed that the doctor needed to come right away, the new born baby was very sick. The doctor's wife explained that the doctor had driven over to Birmingham and would not be home until much later that evening. He would come over the next day. James hurried home to tell Ma Elliott the bad news. Ma Elliott thought, "There won't be any going home tonight. I'll need to stay here all night with this very sick baby!" All night long and into the next day, Ma Elliott administered her form of CPR on the tiny baby. By mid-morning of the next day, there seemed to be some improvement in the infant. What had happened? Why did this baby almost die? It wasn't uncommon for an infant to die at birth back then. Sadly, the cemeteries had more than their share of small, infant grave markers. There was no such thing as prenatal care, no monthly check ups during pregnancy, and no hospital delivery rooms with fresh flowers, fancy curtains, and nurses and doctors monitoring the progress every step of the way.

Over the next month the baby, although still pale and weak, made slow progress and gained strength. It was a mystery why the baby had experienced such distress at birth. It wouldn't be until approximately fifty years later that the mystery would be solved. Prior to 1937, approximately ten thousand babies a year in America were stillborn. Others were born with severe mental retardation. Doctors and scientist were well aware of this malady and were diligently trying to determine the cause of these tragic infant deaths. One year later, in 1937, a major breakthrough was discovered, resulting in literally thousands of babies being saved in future generations.

At about three years of age, I began exploring the great outdoors. It was a wonderful place! So much to see and do. Why would anyone want to stay in the house when there was so much to explore outside? Lois seemed content to stay inside much of the time, playing with her cut-out paper dolls and having Frances and Vera curl her hair. Ugh!

Beginning early in the morning, I would go out on the front porch and watch the sun rise over Dellah's cornfield. I listened to the morning sounds. Ole No. 6 steam engine locomotive was always very prompt. The whistle would begin about three miles east of the small town as the train bore down on the three railroad crossings, two on the east side and one on the west side of the small town. The engineer would blow three long blasts of the whistle, then three very short blasts. The whistle could be easily heard night and day and was used by the ridge people as a clock, due to their reliable schedule through town. Ole No. 6 came through at precisely 6:00 a.m. then No. 12 came through at noon and ole No. 5 came through at precisely 5:00 p.m.

One other came through later at night. Beside the trains, numerous other types of morning noises would greet you each morning. Everyone had chickens and of course roosters. Just before dawn, the hills would reverberate with roosters crowing from all directions. I learned to distinguish the various roosters by their crowing. Generally the McDonald's Rhode Island red rooster would begin the serenade, followed by Monroe's ole Dominecker, then the Files's bantams would join the chorus! Shortly after full daylight, the crowing would stop as if they felt they had done their job and were responsible for ushering in another new day. Occasionally during the day, you could hear a rooster crow but not nearly like at dawn.

In early spring, the mockingbirds would perch high up in the black walnut tree in the front yard and sing incessantly all day and sometimes all night. These birds seemed to be the happiest creatures on earth! Once the female mockingbirds began to nest, however, the males would develop a nasty disposition. They would make a harsh scolding sound if you came near their nest. They would swoop down and attack a dog or cat or a child if they were near their nest. Vera and Lois were very afraid of these mockingbirds when they would swoop down at them. I always thought, "It's only a little bird, what's there to be afraid of?" I've never met a bird I've been afraid of. I often sparred with the barnyard roosters and tom turkeys. I could whip them all!

After a short time, they all learned to leave me alone, but once they learned the girls were afraid of them, they would lie in wait for an opportunity to chase the girls into the house! Early each day the crows would leave their roosting place in the pine trees. They were very destructive and often raided the corn just as it began to mature. They were highly intelligent and all but impossible to sneak upon to try to shoot them. Scarecrows didn't work at all to scare them away. Later, as a teenager, I learned to imitate the distress call of the crows. I would hide in the corn and using my mouth, make the distress call. The whole flock of crows would immediately come swooping in to help chase what they thought was an owl stealing a young crow from its nest. I could see the panic in their eyes as I stood up in the tall corn and shot two or three out of the sky before they could make a rapid retreat.

Quails were very prolific singers or whistlers in the early spring. They were also quite tasty! There was also the constant chatter of various woodpeckers. Early mornings could be very noisy. By noon time, when the hot sun made it uncomfortable to be out, the birds and animals would retreat into the cool shrubs and deep forest to await the cooler evening time.

In the evening, a whole new array of sounds would emerge. All night long the soft relaxing uniform cadence of the crickets would be very soothing and put a child to sleep very quickly. However, the loud ruckus call of the katydid would startle you awake as they landed on the window ledge and then turned up the volume! Night hawks would shriek overhead in the late evening sky. Soon the whippoorwills would chime in with their whip poor will, whip poor will, whip poor will calls. After their incessant calling for about a half hour, they could become very annoying. Hoot owls would hoot for a short time but then be done for the night. Noisy birds and insects disturbed your sleep, but there was no concern for more dangerous animals. There were no wolves, coyotes, bears, or cougars. Apparently the larger animals had been hunted to extinction in this region by the earlier pioneers. One other night sound which disturbed my sleep frequently was our big dog, ole Mickey.

By the time I was four or five years old, mother would allow me to walk alone down to the Atkins house to play with Jody. I also could go up to the McDonalds to play with Henry or go to the Hendrix house to play with Frankie. Mother would say, "When you hear ole No. 12, you come right home." If I was late getting home, Mother would stand out in the yard and yell at the top of her lungs, "Lou-is, Lou-is!" I would hear this call and answer back, "Coming!" Then promptly head home. Tardiness could result in a spanking. Sometimes the three friends would meet up to play, usually by accident. Jody would come to my house and I may have already gone up to the McDonalds to play with Henry. He would then come on up there and then we would decide to go to the Hendrix house to play with Frankie. One of the favorite games to play at the Hendrix house was a game of king of the hill on the large haystacks in their pasture. We would see who could remain on the hay stack the longest without being thrown off.

At age five, our mothers had already given us much liberty to go from house to house to play. Usually her warning would be, "Watch out for snakes and don't play in snaky looking places." Sometimes as we walked along the dirt roads, we would encounter snakes crossing the road. Most of the time ole Mickey was with us and he'd chase the snakes, often catching them. He would shake them very violently, breaking their back bones. He seemed to hate snakes!

One very embarrassing situation occurred when I was about four years old. Early one morning, I went to the outhouse. Once finished, I tried to put my bib overalls back on, but the suspenders had become very tangled and I couldn't seem to get them untangled. I gave up trying and thought I would just go back to the house and let Mother help me. So with overalls in hand and a bare bottom, I started back to the house. Just as I emerged from between the smokehouse and the corn crib, I came face to face with all the Swindle girls on their way to school. They just said good morning like everything was perfectly normal and continued on their way to school. I learned a valuable lesson that day!

Sequel, 1936   1941

In 1937, two doctors named Karl Landsteiner and Alexander Wiener pioneered research which helped solve the mysteries of all these stillborn deaths. Concurrent with other researchers, they determined that a small amino protein matter attached on the red blood cells of mothers who experienced stillborn births was a common factor in all these women. It was classified as the RH negative blood type. This factor is very rare in most races. However, in about 15 percent of Caucasian women, this condition exist. This RH negative blood type is incompatible with blood classified as RH positive blood types. The first or second pregnancies of mothers with the RH negative factor generally pose no risk to the fetus. However, with each pregnancy, a mother's blood will began to build up antibodies in her immune system. Simply by being exposed to the very small amount of blood in the umbilical cord or exposure to the positive blood while giving previous births, it will cause her antibodies to continue to strengthen and multiply in her immune system. These antibodies will then begin attacking the RH positive red blood cells in the fetus's body. It's very similar to when you receive a flu vaccine in early fall, the antibodies will multiply so that within six weeks after the immunization, your body will have built up optimum resistance to the flu. This is why the later pregnancies are far more likely to produce a stillborn baby. The fetus's red blood cells will continually be destroyed by the mother's immune system, reducing the fetus's ability to carry oxygen to its developing cells.

Further research resulted in the development of an anti-RHO immunoglobulin injection, which can be injected into the RH negative mother during the first twenty-eight weeks of pregnancy. This injection will destroy the antibodies in the mother's immune system, and she can then safely and normally carry a RH positive fetus without complications.

Approximately forty years after my birth, my mother had a very severe heart attack. She wasn't expected to live, but she survived and lived another thirty-five years before the fatal car accident in 1979. While being treated by her cardiologist, he noticed in her blood work that she had the RH negative blood type. Frances was sitting in the room when the cardiologist asked Mother if she was aware that she had the negative blood type. Vora stated, "No, I don't know anything about that." He then asked if she had any children. Mother responded, "Yes, I have seven children." He seemed amazed and blurted out, "Are they all right? Mother looked over at Frances and stated, "I reckon they're all right, aren't they, Frances?" I don't think she ever understood why the doctor was so intrigued with the fact she had seven children and they all had survived. The seventh child, however, almost didn't make it! Thankfully with our modern health care system, many infants have been saved from this malady.

Still today, health care is not available to everyone. Adequate health care continues to be a problem in America, especially for the poor. It now has become one of those benefits affordable only by the affluent. In 1979, I assumed the duties of administrator for a medium-sized nursing home complex. One of my first administrative priorities was to secure health insurance for our approximately seventy-five full-time employees. Since our staff was comprised of about 80 percent young women of child bearing age, the insurance representative informed me that our premiums would be significantly more than normal. The premiums were twenty-eight dollars per month for each employee! (No, this isn't a typo!) Today the coverage for this group of young women is approximately five to six hundred dollars each! About twenty times more than it was in 1979. Most poor people cannot afford this, and hence, many remain uninsured. They hope they will remain in good health and not need the health insurance.

There has been much debate in congress during recent years about affordable health care (Affordable Health Care Act.) Small business owners, self-employed individuals, retail merchants, etc. have opposed the federally mandated health insurance requirement. It will potentially hurt their bottom line and will place a significant financial burden on small shop owners. At the same time, single parents with children and families with low paying jobs are relieved with the hope of now getting affordable health insurance for their families.

From 1979 until 2015, health insurance premiums have multiplied twenty times. If a person was making fifteen thousand dollars in 1979, then to maintain this ratio between income and health insurance cost today, he would need to be earning three hundred thousand dollars today! Why have such enormous increases occurred over the past thirty-seven years? Research has placed much of the blame on nonhealth related issues. People are not sicker than they were thirty-seven years ago. Liability insurance premiums for hospitals and doctors cost about $55.6 billion dollars annually in

America. Add another one hundred billion credited to fraud. Then it's anybody's guess as to what the cost is for what is termed defensive medicine, which, admittedly, is being practiced by 93 percent of today's doctors (ordering unnecessary test, treatments, CTs, biopsies, MRIs, etc.) just to protect themselves from law suits. No one knows how to compute this cost, but it must be enormous; a waste of billions upon billions of dollars! If this waste could be eliminated, it would go a long way toward reducing the $2.6 trillion now being spent on health care a year in the United States.

The War Years

Not in so many words, but clearly understood: "You're six years old now, it's time to pull your own weight." No more playing all day with the baby chickens, turkeys, and other farm animals, and no more exploring all day in the forest. You have morning and evening chores. Once the chores are done, if there's enough daylight left, there may be time to go to a friend's house and play. The younger children were responsible for such chores as feeding the chickens and gathering the eggs. The corn was always stored in the corn crib still in the dry husk. In the evening, Lois and I were assigned the task of husking about three dozen ears of corn, then running it through a hand cranked corn sheller. Once the corn was removed off the cob, it was then scooped into a gallon bucket and taken to feed the chickens. The shelled corn was simply scattered on the ground for the chickens and turkeys to eat.

A six-year-old boy was expected to be able to carry a twenty-pound bucket of coal into the house. Since we cooked with coal as well as using it for heat, it required about sixty pounds of coal a day for the stove and fireplaces (less in the summer time.) Kindling wood also had to be cut and split into thin strips to get the fires started. We usually searched the pine forest for the pine knots and rosin-rich dead branches to use as kindling wood. Rosin was the gummy pine sap which could be easily set on fire with a match. It burned very hot and that, in turn, would get the coal burning quickly.

Sometimes on Saturdays, Fred and I would hitch our newly acquired horse, ole Dolly, to the wagon and go to the extreme western end of the property to gather pine knots and other wood suitable for kindling wood. Once while chopping the branches into stove length to load into the wagon, Fred took a mighty swing with the axe onto a well-seasoned hickory log which was very, very hard. The axe glanced off the hickory log and struck Fred squarely on the big toe of his high top shoe. He yelled and fell to the ground moaning and rolling in pain. Being some distance away, I called out, "Fred, what happened?" He responded, "I just chopped my big toe off." I quickly ran over to where Fred was, still moaning and rolling on the ground. I gently unlaced the shoe and very gently started to slip the shoe off his foot. I full expected to see a shoe full of blood and a severed big toe. To my amazement, there was not even a scratch on his toe, nor was there any blood! Fred has been known to exaggerate from time to time!

The mules, Frank and Beck, had gotten old and they both had died. James felt really bad about Frank's death. He had plowed him the day before and the ole mule kept braying all day long. James kept swatting him with the plow line whenever he would bray. That night he died in his stable. After the mules died, Dad bought a young horse about two years old, which had never been broken for plowing or pulling a wagon. She was a beautiful light-brown colored mare and we named her Dolly. Dad spent the better part of the summer training Dolly how to plow. Instead of pulling, as was expected of her, Dolly would refuse to pull the plow and would often back up, even backing into the plow and getting all tangled up in the harnesses and plow chains. One day, becoming tired of these antics, Dad tied a pitch fork to the plow so that if Dolly backed up she would get a good jab in her rump from the pitch fork tines. Very soon Dolly learned it was far less painful to go forward than backward!

Dolly was very gentle, and I would often sit on her in the pasture while she grazed without a bridle or reins on her. Once when Jody and I were both sitting on Dolly in the pasture, a mean older brother popped Dolly in the rump with a BB gun. She ran full bore into the pine thicket, knocking Jody and me off as she ran under a big pine tree limb. Sometimes we would take Dolly swimming with us. She loved the water. She would swim just like the kids. She would paw the water so aggressively that she would muddy the entire swimming hole and our swimming would be done for the day!

One morning, Mother was sitting on the front porch snapping green beans for lunch. Dolly was in the pasture right in front of the house. Several of us kids were playing with ole Mickey, tossing a ball and playing keep-a-way. The dog was barking and the kids were yelling and running. Dolly apparently decided she wanted to get in on the fun. She began to run in the pasture, then suddenly she kicked her hind legs high up in the air and simultaneously let out a very loud toot! Mother became hysterical with laughter. As children, we didn't quite know what to do, but seeing Mother laughing so hysterically, we broke into laughter as well.

Usually on Thanksgiving weekend, we would hitch Dolly to the wagon and go deep into the forest using old logging trails. We would be searching for Christmas trees, holly, and mistletoe. Usually during our summertime excursions in the forest, we would select the tree we would chop down for our Christmas tree. Since pine trees were so common, we much preferred finding a cedar tree. They weren't very common, and when we found one, we did not dare let other ridge children know its location. Otherwise it probably would be gone when we went for it. When searching for Christmas decorations and trees, we usually would leave right after breakfast and not return until late afternoon. The forest was full of things to eat, and we didn't pack a lunch. There were hickory nuts, black walnuts, and wild pecans. By day's end, each child would have an old flour sack full of nuts they had gathered, in addition to all they had smashed between two flat rocks and eaten.

Wild grape we called muskedines were abundant in the fall. These grapes were about the size of marbles and grew on large vines which often reached the tops of tall trees. Wild persimmons were also abundant but were very sour until a frost came. Then they would turn sweet and delicious. Wild asparagus was also plentiful in the early spring. Wild plums, pears, and apple trees grew around the edges of fields. This was probably the results of opossums, raccoons, and squirrels stealing the fruit from farms and leaving the seeds to sprout in a new location. The children also knew the location of clean water which bubbled up from the ground in cool flowing streams. There was no concern about drinking this water, and it was always so refreshing and cold.

Shortly after Thanksgiving, it was hog killing weather and corn gathering time. Dad would always wait until there were several frosty days in a row before slaughtering the hogs. One or two neighbors or relatives would assist with the hog killing. The animal was shot right between the eyes and then one of the men would jump into the pen and slit its throat to allow the hog to properly bleed. A big sixty gallon drum was filled with boiling water, and the hog was placed into the hot water to loosen the hair on its body. Then it would be hung up by its hind legs to be gutted. Once this was completed, the carcass would be cut up into its respective pieces, hams, shoulders, chops, side meat, and roast. The fat was all trimmed off and placed in a big pot over a fire to "render" out the lard. The lard was then saved in large containers for frying and seasoning almost everything eaten. All the meat was cooled down and then placed in the large salt box inside the smoke house. The meat had to be totally buried in the salt to keep it from spoiling. Of course the pig brains would be scrambled with eggs the next morning for a delicious breakfast. The pig's feet would be pickled in a vinegar solution for a few weeks, then thoroughly enjoyed at a later meal! The children all enjoyed hog killing time. Fresh pork chops fried a golden brown in a cast iron skillet with brown gravy and mashed potatoes just couldn't be beat!

The corn was now ready to be gathered. This was all done manually by the children; no mechanical corn picker! The corn had to be picked by hand and then stored in the corn crib to be used to feed the chickens, turkeys, and horse during the winter months. Dolly would be hitched to the wagon and with three rows of corn on the left, two rows directly under the wagon, and three more rows on the right side of the wagon, the horse and wagon would began moving through the corn patch. One child would manually pull all the corn in the three left rows, one would pull the two rows directly behind the wagon, and the third child would pull all the corn in the three right rows. Once you had your arms full, you would take your arm load of corn over to the wagon and dump it in. When you had gathered all the corn right up to the horse's head, then you would tell Dolly to get up, and she would move forward through the corn until you gave the command whoa. She would stop, and the picking process would start all over again. The most difficult rows to pick were the two rows directly behind the wagon. These rows would be crushed down and tangled up from having the wagon running over them. Once the wagon was full, the corn would be taken to the corn crib to be unloaded. This required two operations: first the corn had to be tossed by hand up into the corn crib through the door. Then two children inside the corn crib would have to throw the corn deeper into the corn crib to allow room for the next load needing to be unloaded. By day's end, your fingers would be cut, swollen, and sore from ripping all the corn from the stalks. Usually we needed approximately three hundred bushels of corn stored for winter's use to feed the chickens and horse. A special ground up feed was bought for the pigs and milk cow. Apparently these animals cannot grind up the hard corn with their teeth. The horse had no problem chewing the hard corn. Dolly made a loud grinding noise as she chewed the dried corn right off the cob. You could hear her grinding away all the way from the barn to the house.

The horse stall, cow stall, and the chicken coop would be filled with corn cobs, dried hay, and manure by spring. This was highly valued as fertilizer for the vegetable garden. Each spring, the manure had to be cleaned from the stables and chicken coop and then spread on the site where the vegetable garden would be planted. Using a shovel and pitch fork, the manure was scooped up into a wheel barrow and then wheeled out to the garden site and evenly spread over the site. Then the turning plow would be used to turn the soil over, burying the manure into the soil. I never minded this task at all. The manure was considered a valuable commodity, and the more you had, the more likely you were to having an outstanding vegetable garden.

During the war years, money was still scarce and commercial fertilizer for the fields of corn was very expensive. The chemicals used for fertilizer were greatly needed for making explosives for war use. Hence, there was a very limited allotment of fertilizer for each farmer. Instead of using the corn planter which was pulled by a mule, Dad utilized his children instead to conserve on fertilizer. The planter would distribute a steady stream of fertilizer in the furrow being planted. It would also drop a liberal amount of corn seeds. Instead of using this planter, Lois and I had to drop the fertilizer and seeds by hand, one hill at a time. I would pour the fertilizer into a five gallon pail and drop a handful of fertilizer about every foot in the furrow. Lois would then come along behind and drop two kernels of corn beside each handful of fertilizer. This was a very large field, and Lois and I felt it would take about a hundred years to get it all planted. As we got toward the end of the day, sometimes Lois would run out of corn. Then we could quit a little early. Unfortunately when the corn began to sprout, Dad found out why Lois had run out of corn much sooner than he expected. Large clumps of corn were sprouting up where Sissy had secretly buried it! We were seven years old at this time.

Since there was no kindergarten, Lois and I didn't start school until September 1942. Fred had sounded a warning, "You better hope you don't get Miss Hollis for a teacher. She's really mean." The first year Lois and I began going to school was the first time the ridge children were included on a school bus route. We waited at the end of our lane until we saw the school bus coming up the main road. We were very excited to get to go to school. Lois and I had both learned much already from listening to Vera and Fred recite their lessons in the evening. The school was very big on memory work. Once when Mother was writing a letter to James, who was now in the army, she asked me if I would like to write a note to James which she would include with her letter. I said yes and Mother gave me a pencil and piece of paper. After thinking a few minutes, I asked Mother, "How do you spell hell?" Mother gasped, jumped up and exclaimed, "Louis, what are you writing?" I responded, "I'm trying to spell hello, and I already know how to spell O!" She was much relieved by this explanation.

Frances and Vera got off the school bus with Lois and I that first day of school. We were led into a room full of other children and their parents. I began admiring the neat desk with the storage compartment underneath the desk top. When the teacher entered the room, she stated, "Children, my name is Miss Hollis!" I felt like running out of the room, remembering how Fred had described Miss Hollis as very, very mean. I wondered if Fred had also told the little girl sitting next to me how mean Ms. Hollis was because she peed her pants big time!

After being in her class for a few weeks, I learned Ms. Hollis was not nearly as mean as Fred had described. I should have learned by then not to listen to Fred. One evening in the late spring, Dad had directed Fred to plow the upper ten-acre field of corn the next day. Fred got up early, ate his breakfast, and then hitched ole Dolly to the plow and went to the field to begin plowing the corn. By now, midmorning could be very warm and humid. About 10:00., Mother told me to draw a bucket of fresh, cool water from the well and take Fred a cool drink. I drew the water and filled an empty gallon fruit jar with the water to take to Fred. As I got to the ten-acre cornfield, I looked for Fred and ole Dolly. I saw neither out in the field. I looked over at the edge of the field where several large oak and hickory trees were growing. I saw Dolly standing in the shade of the trees and Fred was lying on the ground. I quickly ran toward them, fearing some-thing was wrong with Fred. Once I reached him, Fred was obviously very sick. He was sweating profusely and his face was ashen colored, and just as I arrived, he rolled over and heaved mightily, "So sick." I asked Fred what was wrong and he said, "I took a big chaw of tobacco about an hour ago and now I'm dying!" I looked on the ground by one of the trees and spotted a big plug of Red Man chewing tobacco. One big bite was missing from the plug. I began to laugh. Fred said, "If I wasn't so sick, I'd beat the snot out of you." Fred tried to throw up again, but by now it was only dry heaves! I told Fred to go home and go to bed and I'd take care of Ole Dolly. Fred slowly got up, reached down for the Red Man tobacco, and with a mighty throw, sent it out of sight down the hillside. I stifled my laughter and started unhitching Ole Dolly from the plow as Fred made his way home. He stayed in bed all day long, and that evening when Dad came home, Mother told Dad what had happened. Dad scolded Fred and said, "By Ned, one of these days you'll learn to listen to me and not mess with tobacco." Dad pulled his pouch of Prince Albert smoking tobacco from his pocket and proceeded to pack his pipe with the tobacco. I chuckled at this paradox. "Do as I say, not as I do!"

One Friday afternoon, after working in the fields all day, Vera, Fred, Lois, and I along with some other ridge chil-dren decided to go swimming. We decided to go down to a place on the larger creek we called Icy Doe. This was where the small stream in the valley belonging to Jim Delevecheo emptied into the larger creek. Along this small stream were two or three artesian springs which bubbled up from deep within the ground. These springs made Icy Doe much colder than the typical creek water. Icy Doe was also much larger and deeper than most of the other swimming holes. As we got fairly near Icy Doe, Fred and I ran ahead of the other children so we would be the first to get in the water. When we got to the swimming hole, we spied a flat bottom wooden row boat lodged among the reeds by the shore. It had apparently broken free from its mooring somewhere up stream and had become stuck against the shore at Icy Doe. Fred immediately jumped into the boat which still had a single paddle in it, and naturally, I jumped in as well to get a boat ride. Fred shoved the boat away from shore and began to paddle it out into the water.

When we had gotten about ten feet away from shore, the other children arrived. Fred looked down into the bottom of the boat and there was a small geyser of water spurting up from a small hole. He started yelling to the other children, "Help, there's a leak! We're going to sink!" Not knowing how to swim, I looked back and thought if I could make a mighty leap, I could almost jump back to the shore. I stood up and launched myself out of the boat toward shore. Perhaps I would have made it except for the fact that "For every action there is an equal and opposite reaction." As I sprang out of the boat, most of my kicking energy simply propelled the boat further out into the water behind me, and I sank almost straight down right behind the boat. The water was well over my head, and I immediately sank right to the bottom. I then kicked up from the bottom and propelled myself straight back up to the surface. I immediately sank back to the bottom and once again propelled myself back up to the surface of the water. As I sank for the third time, I began to think, "If I don't learn to swim right now, I'm probably going to drown!" I remembered how Vera had been trying to teach me how to swim. I instinctively remembered how she had tried to get me to lay out on the surface of the water and kick my feet and dog paddle with my hands. I thought, "When I reach the surface this next time, I'll try to do that." When my head reached the surface, I laid out on the top of the water and began to dog paddle. Hallelujah! I began to swim! As I dog paddled toward shore, I looked over to my right and saw Vera swimming next to me. She had swam out to try and save me! Needless to say, I stayed very close to shore the remainder of that trip.

One nice warm morning in the fall of 1942, I asked Mother if I could go to Frankie's to play. She gave her usual warning, "Watch out for snakes and come home when you hear ole No. 12's whistle." I started up the road and then took Oscar Meyer's shortcut through the woods to his house. This was about one-fourth mile shorter than walking the road. Just as I emerged from the woods right into the yard of Kate and Oscar's place, I heard Aunt Kate wailing and screaming hysterically. She was screaming, "Oh no, oh no!" over and over again. I was frozen in my tracks. Chills began to run up and down my spine. I'd never before experienced such grief in my short life. There was a police car parked in her front yard. A man in military uniform and the policeman were on the porch with Aunt Kate trying to console her. They had just delivered the official telegram which begins: "I regret to inform you that your son, Oscar Dugan Meyers was killed in action..."

Still standing there, not knowing what to do, I looked and saw Mother running up the road toward Aunt Kate's. Mother had seen the police car pass our house. She was very, very relieved that it hadn't turned into our lane because she knew that the police only ventured this far out of town to deliver bad news. Since it didn't turn up the lane toward our house, she thought it must surely be going to Kate and Oscar's. Mother ran upon the porch and wept bitterly as she hugged Aunt Kate. I remained frozen in the yard. After several minutes, Aunt Kate's weeping subsided somewhat. Mother looked out in the yard and saw me still standing there. She came over where I was standing and simply said, "Don't go to Frankie's. I want you to go home." I started back home.

What began as a nice warm morning had turned into a sad day. My skin felt clammy and my legs seemed to quiver from experiencing this emotional scene. Just inside the woods near where our lane intersected with the main road was a large flat rock. It was a place I would sometimes go to sit and listen to the forest noises. It seemed to beckon me that morning. I went over and sat on that rock and wept. I thought, "Who is this evil man named Hitler and why is he trying to kill us?" I'd seen pictures in the newspaper depicting Hitler wearing the heavy, odd shaped German helmet and having a tiny little mustache and evil looking eyes. Sometimes, Frankie, Jody, and I would cut his picture out of the newspaper and nail it on the side of the barn. We would then shoot at it with our BB gun. A direct hit right between those evil eyes would elicit a shout and much jumping up and down! I thought about where we could hide if Hitler's soldiers came after us. Could we escape by running deep into the forest? Maybe we could hide in one of the old abandoned mines. What if we couldn't hide and they came and jabbed their bayonets into our bellies until they exited all the way through our backs! Why was this terrible war happening? I just didn't know; so much to wonder about at six years old.

The news about Dugan's death spread rapidly from one end of the ridge to the other. By word of mouth, every home was informed. All the ridge folks came over to sit with Kate and Oscar. They brought food. Some sat on the porch, others sat out in the yard, and some sat all night. Mother came home to cook supper for Jonny and the children. Her grief had now begun to turn to worry. Her second oldest, James, who was also Dugan's best buddy, was over in Europe fighting the Nazis. "Lord, please, please keep him safe!"

The mood among the ridge folks turned very somber. Monroe stopped whistling for a few weeks. The crowing of the rooster's seemed to take on a mournful sound early each morning. Even the dogs lay calmly on their porches as people passed by. They seemed to sense a loss among the ridge people. The ridge people were all like family.

Just before James was shipped overseas in 1942, somehow by sheer coincidence, both James and John Jr. came home on leave at the same time. John Jr. had hitchhiked all the way from California. It was easy for a young man in uniform to hitch a ride. It took John Jr. about three days to hitchhike from California to Alabama. He told how the first day he had made it across to the pan-handle area of Texas. Since traffic was very light after midnight, he camped out' overnight with a group of hobos. They had a fire going and he kept warm all night by sleeping near the fire. Early the next morning, he got back on the road hitchhiking to Alabama. He noticed everyone looking at him strangely. Finally when he looked into a large rear view mirror of a truck, he saw his face was black from the soot from the fire. He arrived home three days after leaving California. James was already home. Someone took a picture of the whole Elliott clan during the time they were home on leave.

John Jr. and James decided to go into the small town for a visit during their time at home. Just for fun, they decided to switch uniforms. John Jr. put on James's army uniform and James put on John Jr.'s navy uniform. As luck would have it, when they got into town, two military policemen stopped them and checked their credentials. Being thoroughly confused by the uniform exchange, the MP's took several minutes sorting everything out. They demanded James and John Jr. go somewhere immediately and exchange uniforms. The boys went to Ma Rosie's and changed back into their proper uniforms.

During the war years, there were many troop trains which came through the small town. Many had to stop to take on more water and coal. The young soldiers would hang their heads out all the windows and talk with the town people. Young girls would run over to the train depot and talk with the soldiers. The soldiers seemed happy and were smiling because of all the attention they were receiving. They didn't seem to worry about where they were headed. The train traffic became very heavy. Not only was there numerous troop trains but many trains came through loaded with tanks, army trucks, and jeeps. The highway was also very heavily traveled. Many convoys of military vehicles were being driven through the small town. Above the ridge, there were numerous squadrons of large planes flying over in formation. The children would always count how many were in each squadron. Most times there would be eighteen to twenty planes flying in very close formation. They usually came from the southwest and were traveling toward the northeast.

The government began a campaign for everyone to collect any and all scrap metal and bring it to a collection center in the small town. Tin cans, old rusty farm implements, and especially any scrap copper or brass were readily accepted. Schools began to sell war stamps to the children. Each week a child would purchase a five- or ten-cent stamps which they pasted in a booklet. After the booklet was filled, it could be redeemed at a later date for the full face value plus interest. Due to the war, many items were placed on ration by the government. Each person was allowed an allotment of things like gasoline each month. Once they had used up their allotment, they were without gasoline for the remainder of the month. Rubber products were not available, all the rubber was restricted for military use. Most other types of manufactured goods were very difficult to buy.

The Galloway Coal company store was still in business during the war years. Their script money was still being utilized. On Saturdays, Jody, Frankie, and I would go down to the small town and look for script tokens in the alleys and the curbs along the front street. It took five tokens to equal a penny. Sometimes miners would simply toss the tokens in the gutter rather than bother with them. If we were lucky, we might find enough tokens to buy an ice cream cone.

Jonny had fairly steady work during the war years. However, most items needing to be purchased had become much more expensive. He was, however, able to purchase his first vehicle. It was an old Ford truck of about 1935 vintage. It was all beat up and rusty but still ran. If the weather appeared to possibly be below freezing at night, then Jonny would have to empty the water from the radiator in the evening and then refill it the next morning. Antifreeze was very expensive and also very difficult to find because of the war. The old truck had a dead battery as well. There was no replacement available. Each evening, Jonny would park the old truck at the top of the hill leading from our house down to the main road. In the morning, he would manually give it a shove down the lane. Once it was coasting fairly well he would jump into the truck and put it in gear, which would start the engine. I assume he had a similar hill near the mine where he worked so he could get it started again in the evening when he was ready to come home.

Germany and her allies proved to be a formable opponent at the onset of the war. Frequently on the radio, the news was very bad. Germany was marching across Europe at an alarming rate. Everyone was deeply concerned. A tense and anxious mood engulfed the entire nation.

In spite of the war, life went on in the ridge community. The children still did their chores and found time to play. Once while waiting for Dad to transact some business with a family living about twelve miles east of us, I observed a flock of ducks in their yard. The man said the duck eggs were bigger and tasted better than chicken eggs. He gave me about six duck eggs and suggested we have them for breakfast the next morning. He also showed me how to build a rabbit trap. The next morning, Mother said she didn't want to eat any duck eggs. There was a brooding hen in our chicken coop which decided to quit laying and began to sit on a nest. She stubbornly continued to sit on an empty nest, trying to incubate some imaginary eggs. I decided to place the duck eggs under this brooding hen. She very faithfully sat on these duck eggs and successfully hatched them. She was very protective of her brood of babies, and the baby ducklings followed her just as if she were their real mother. Everything was fine, until one day we had a very heavy downpour of rain. The rain filled some ruts in the road with water. The baby ducklings found these water puddles and dived right in. They were having a great time swimming and dipping their heads under water. Mother hen didn't know what to do. She was clucking, squawking, and flapping her wings, trying to get her strange chicks out of the puddles!

The rabbit trap design proved to be very effective. I built two traps and caught many rabbits. Every morning before going to school, I would check my rabbit traps. Usually there would be at least one rabbit in one of the traps. Sometimes there would be an opossum or even a skunk in the trap! Once I caught the Atkins's ole cat. The trap didn't hurt the animals, it just had a door which would drop when a trigger was tripped which would prevent the animal from escaping. Apparently, one time I must have caught a squirrel. A big hole was gnawed in the door and it escaped.

Jody, Frankie, and I continued to have play time together. One of our pastimes was collecting Indian arrowheads, fossils found on coal, and animal bones. In the springtime, when the ground was being turned over for planting, we would find many arrowheads. Most children had a sizeable collection of arrowheads. We would often trade if someone else had one we liked. I had an old gallon syrup bucket almost full of Indian arrowheads. I wondered if these arrowheads were there as a result of a battle between Indian tribes, or if they were just from hundreds of years of hunting wild game.

Many large chunks of coal would have fossils on their surface. Small worms, some centipede types of fossils, ferns, and other types of fossilized plants could be found on the coal. We looked for the fossil with the most detail and the ones best preserved. Most were only about the size of the palm of your hand. We would also trade these fossils with other children. The bone collection wasn't nearly as important. Mostly we collected skulls found of small animals and birds. We would often argue over the identity of these small skulls.

One day, I was walking along the main road toward Frankie's house. John McDonald and his oldest son, Charles, were destroying a crow's nest high up in a pine tree. Charles was up in the tree, and he was throwing baby crows down and John was killing them. I asked John if he would give me one of the baby crows. He let me take one home with me. It was an ugly little critter, mostly bare reddish colored skin with some scraggly feathers. I decided I would call it Moe. I mixed raw milk and hog feed together to form a mush and fed this to Moe. He loved the food and grew very rapidly.

Within two months, he was able to fly. He stayed outside in the trees but would always come when he was called. In the early morning, Moe would often perch on the roof just above the back door, waiting for his food. One morning, Dad stepped out the back door, and Moe immediately flew down, knocking Dad's hat off and his pipe out of his mouth. Dad was very upset! He came back inside and said, "That blame crow almost scared me to death!" After being around for about a year, one morning Moe flew down into the chicken yard and our big ole Rhode Island Red rooster attacked him. A well-aimed spur to the head killed pore ole Moe. I didn't miss him much; he was too noisy early every morning, and he had gotten to be a pest anytime I was outside.

We always looked forward to summertime and no school. Unfortunately if the summer was hot and extremely dry, the creeks would dry up and become stagnant. It was not suitable for swimming. Mother would always warn us not to go swimming in the stagnant water. It was suspected this might be the source of the dreaded disease called polio. This disease was responsible for many deaths among young children as well as crippling many more. Every child and their parents lived in fear of contracting this horrible disease. I knew one child my age who survived polio. He was paralyzed on the entire right side of his body. He was able to ambulate with the assistance of heavy metal braces on his right leg. His right arm was useless and was carried in a sling. His mouth was pulled to one side, and he could not control his drool. He could form words, and if you listened carefully, you could understand what he was saying. His name was Charles Tipper. Some of the children befriended Charles and would play with him during recess. Charles would chase us dragging that useless right leg through the dirt. We'd let him catch us, and he would whack us across the back or shoulders using his left hand. We would scream like he was really beating us up, and Charles would laugh with delight. After the fifth grade, Charles disappeared. I don't know if he moved or just what happened to him. Fearing polio, we didn't take any risk and stayed out of the creeks during the hot dry summer months.

When I was about seven years old, I asked Mother if I could go down to Jody's to play. She said I could go, and as I started down the road, I could see a large black cloud of smoke rising up near the Atkins home. I thought someone was burning some trash or a pile of brush. Before I could actually see the house, however, Delmer came running down the road from Dellah's house toward her own house. I started running toward the Atkins house, and when I could see it, I could see flames shooting out the roof at the kitchen end of the house. It was too late for anyone to do anything about it. We simply stood there and watched the flames totally engulf the house in a matter of minutes. Several neighbors had been attracted by the smoke. They knew it was most likely a barn or house burning. No one could do anything except watch as the entire house burned to the ground. I don't know where Jody and Delmar stayed for the next several days. About a week later, they came by our house to say good-bye. I asked Jody where they were going, and he tried to be excited about the move. He stated they were going to move to Chicago where Luke and Dick lived. Among the ridge people, you seldom said good-bye. I simply said to Jody, "I'll see yea." Jody responded, "Yea, I'll see yea." I never saw him again.

The war years were unkind to the small town people and the ridge people. All the young men were drafted into the military and the lure of well-paying jobs in the industrial north attracted others away, seeking a better quality of life.

Sequel: World War II

World War II was fought between 1939 and 1945. It was the bloodiest war in the history of mankind. Nazi Germany, Fascist Italy, and Japan were opposed by Great Britain, France, China, Russia, and the United States. The United States alone suffered 405,399 known military causalities. Many others remained unaccounted for. In total, after the invasion of Pearl Harbor in December 1941, the United States had 16,112,506 military personnel fighting during these four years of conflict. This was the first time in warfare history that there were more civilian causalities than military. Historians tell us there were over one hundred million civilians from thirty different countries who died during this war. Horrific bombing raids killed over one million civilians in France and Germany alone. It is estimated that approximately eleven million Jews were slaughtered by Hitler during World War II. Russia alone suffered approximately twenty million civilian and military causalities. Germany advanced to within fifty miles from Moscow before being beaten back by the Russian army. The very bitterly cold and snowy winter resulted in Germany's long distant supply line being disabled. Russia, with the utilization of American manufactured war supplies, was able to stop the advance of Germany toward their capital. Germany's ranks were also stretched thin by the expanding American forces into Belgium and France. The United States amassed huge numbers of troops in preparation for the invasion of Normandy. Strategic bombing of Germany and Japan's military factories, ships, and railroads eventually led to Germany being incapable of sustaining their war efforts. Germany unconditionally surrendered in May 1945. Then in August, two atomic bombs were dropped on Hiroshima, Japan (August 6, 1945), and Nagasaki, Japan (August 9, 1945). These bombs totally destroyed both cities, resulting in untold causalities and almost a 100 percent obliteration of both cities' population.

In his book entitled, *How American Businesses Produced Victory in World War II*, the author and historian Arthur Herman describes numerous innovative outcomes of American businesses which resulted in creating enormous advantages for the American military. Militarily speaking, many new war concepts and strategies evolved from World War II.

1. The much more rapid deployment of military supplies and equipment by air lifts and parachute drops was first utilized in World War II.
2. Strategic bombing of specific targets greatly crippled Germany's capacity to manufacture needed war equipment.
3. Sophisticated radar was developed, which helped tremendously in navigation and identification of enemy deployment of troops planes and ships.
4. Air craft carriers replaced battleships, which enhanced precision air attacks on enemy targets.

5. Heavy, slow armored and clumsy tanks were replaced with lighter, faster, and more maneuverable tanks with lighter but stronger alloyed armor.
6. Sonar was invented to help track down enemy submarines.
7. New innovative manufacturing techniques resulted in a dramatic reduction of time and money required to produce war goods.

After the war ended, many of the new war inventions were incorporated into peacetime applications. For the first time in history, the government began awarding huge contracts to private corporations for further research and development of many new products. Most notably were:

1. Digital computing: Internet and global positioning systems.
2. Television.
3. Jet engines—Development of rockets.
4. Plastics which were utilized as substitutes for metal.
5. Medical advances such as advances in blood transfusions, blood plasma transfusions in combat, and great advances in utilizing antibiotics such as penicillin.
6. Super strength adhesives and high strength metals such as titanium were developed.
7. Development of cardboard containers capable of holding liquids and able to withstand abuse which would shatter glass containers.
8. New building materials such as plywood, fiberglass, and synthetic rubber.

9. Advances in food preparation, preservation, storage, and balanced nutrition.
10. New more effective training techniques utilizing audio-visual aides, training manuals, and step-by-step sequences.
11. For the first time in history, women were utilized as a new source of labor in manufacturing plants.
12. Amazingly, even fashion was dictated by war needs priorities. In order to conserve on material, the mini skirt was introduced as a fashion trend, which saved much material for war use.

One of the most dreaded after effects of World War II was the introduction of the Cold War. For forty-six years after the end of the war, people lived with the eminent threat of their homeland being totally obliterated off the face of the earth by atomic warfare. Joseph Stalin, czar of Russia, just like Hitler, desired to expand the Russian empire throughout Eastern Europe and beyond. His land grabbing invasion of small Eastern European countries after the war ended, created tension, and anxiety among the free world. How short was his memory! Were it not for the free world coming to his rescue during the war, supplying him with weapons and equipment, it could have very well been that Russia would have being conquered, dissected, chopped up, and plundered by Nazi Germany. What will be our future generations' destructive holocaust? Why not try peaceful coexistence for a change?

War Ends: 1945

As the war wound down in late 1945 and early 1946, all the young soldiers began arriving back home. Bud Inman, E. J. Files, John Jr. and James Elliott, Clarence and J. W. Hendrix, and the two Thornbro brothers down in Bynum Camp. They were all treated as local heroes and rightly so. Jim Thornbro had been severely wounded in the war. He was in a tank division and their tank was disabled either by a land mine or by anti-tank artillery. As Jim and the others bailed out of the disabled tank, they were greeted by Nazi machine gun fire. Jim was hit three times in the back. He fell to the ground and played dead until dark. Somehow none of the bullets struck any vital organs, and after dark, Jim was able to crawl away from the battlefield back into American held territory. Bob Thornbro was in the air force and served as a tail gunner on B-17 and B-29 bombers. He flew numerous missions, and both Jim and Bob received many combat metals and ribbons for their bravery and military service. As the young soldiers came home, there were no jobs for them in the small town. All the major coal mines were now shut down. Strip mining had already extracted most all the coal which was near the surface in the valleys. The beautiful valleys now looked like the surface of the moon. Large craters were left to fill with water. Mounds of broken rock and slag debris were piled randomly all over the valley floor. The valleys were now totally unsuitable for farming.

Unfortunately, the post-war industrial boom did not extend into the small town. There were no new industries, no manufacturing plants, or commercial businesses which chose the small town as their home base. Almost all the soldiers coming home from the war were forced to move on. Some enrolled in college, some even returned to finish high school, and others migrated to northern states like Michigan and Illinois where they found work in the expanding automobile manufacturing industry. The Thornbro brothers left home to settle in the Detroit area. They both found work in the construction industry.

Homes could not be built fast enough to accommodate the hordes of people moving to the well- paying jobs in the Detroit area. Families from Alabama, Tennessee, Kentucky, and West Virginia began swarming into the northern cities. Jim and Bob were two from their family of nine children which comprised the Thornbro clan. Unfortunately their father had died in the early 1940s, leaving these two older boys primarily responsible for looking after the other children. When they moved north, they eventually brought all but one of the nine with them. The youngest of the clan, Charles, Clarence, and Peggy as well as the mother, Mattie, were moved to the Detroit area in 1951.

Circumstances became more difficult for Jonny and Vora. The two older boys left the farm and enrolled as students at Auburn University. Unfortunately the two younger boys, Fred and Louis, were not yet old enough to replace John Jr. and James in the fields. With Fred being sickly, Vora didn't want him doing heavy work in the fields in the hot sun. Louis was only eleven and not yet capable of operating a mule and turning plow all day. Jonny was now no longer capable of working in the mines all day and then coming home to continue working in the fields until dark. The thirty-seven years he had already worked in the mine had begun to take its toll on his body. He was crippled in his back, legs, and hands from arthritis caused by all the time spent in the cold damp conditions found in the mines. His hands were gnarled, with swollen joints and severely twisted fingers. Large sores on the back of his hands never seemed to heal from all the abrasions and scrapes suffered while working in the mines.

While still working for Ole Man Taylor in the small push mines, Jonny was unable to hold his own against the younger, more healthy miners. He began to work less and less in the mines. Since the bottom land had been stripped mined, and no longer suitable for farming, there was less land available for farming.

The homestead was still plagued with hobo types who would sneak in after dark and steal fresh corn, vegetables from the garden, and chickens from the hen house. Once when it was just getting dark, we heard a commotion coming from the hen house. Dad grabbed the shotgun off the bedroom wall, loaded a shell in it, and ran out into the backyard and fired a shot straight up into the air. I wandered what good that would do, but Dad stated, "I don't want to kill nobody over a chicken." Shortly before the Atkins house burned, a stray pregnant dog crawled up under their front porch and had a litter of puppies. The porch was built very close to the ground with only about twelve inches of clearance between the floor and ground. The children would lie on their bellies and look under the porch to see the little puppies. The mother dog would run away but stand a safe distance away, very concerned about her puppies. After about four weeks, I decided to ask Mother and Dad if we could have one of the puppies. Mother stated, "We don't need any more mouths to feed around here." Dad suggested, however, that we could use a guard dog around the place to ward off the thieves and keep the prowlers out of the hen house.

Eventually Mother gave in and allowed us to take one of the puppies. I crawled up under the floor and selected a white puppy with large black spots on his back. Fred and I took it home in a shoe box. It was just beginning to crawl, and we had to hand feed it a few more weeks before it was old enough to eat on its own. We decided to name him Mickey. Mickey grew very rapidly, and we knew he would be a large dog. He was very muscular. He had broad shoulders, powerfully built legs, and a large head and muzzle. Within a year he probably weighed about sixty pounds. He turned out to be a fine guard dog. Unless you were personally acquainted with ole Mickey, you didn't dare come within one hundred yards of our house. Of course he recognized all the regulars who used the path through the cow pasture daily and never showed any concern for their presence. It was a different story however for strangers. He would hold any person he didn't recognize at bay until some of us would call him off and allow the stranger to pass. When I was about ten years old, ole Mickey became my constant companion, whether I liked it or not. Wherever I went, Mickey would always follow along. I didn't like him following me into town when I took the milk, butter, and eggs to Ma Rosie. Many times he would get into fights with other dogs in town.

Most of the time, there would be two or three town dogs who would gang up on ole Mickey. The fights could be very vicious, and Mickey had numerous tears and slits in his ears as a result of these fights. Since Mickey was usually outnumbered by the town dogs, I often would join in the fight, kicking and hitting the other dogs as best I could while still holding the milk and butter. Even outnumbered, Mickey and I would usually send the pack of dogs running with their tails between their legs. It was hopeless to try and discourage Mickey from always following me into town. I would yell, "Mickey, go home!" or "Mickey, git," but he would only lag far enough back so that I had no choice but to allow him to follow. I suppose he sensed that it was his duty to be my protector on these almost daily trips into town to take something to Ma Rosie or else go to the store for Mother. Almost daily, when I got off the school bus at home, Mother would give me eleven cents and send me right back down to the store to get a fresh loaf of bread for the next day's lunches. Sometimes Mother would send eggs with me to sell to the grocery store owner. They generally sold for about sixty cents per dozen or five cents each (exactly the same price of an ice cream cone!)

One day as I started to the store with a dozen eggs to sell, I looked in the hen house and found a freshly lain egg. I took the extra egg to the store and used the extra five cents to buy an ice cream cone. As I stood outside the grocery store enjoying my ice cream cone, Dad stopped at the store to buy some Prince Albert smoking tobacco. He saw me with the ice cream and without even offering me a ride home, he left me eating the ice cream. When he got home, Mother asked him if he had seen me, since she knew I was on the road somewhere. He stated, "I saw him reared back eating an ice cream cone at kitchen's grocery store!" When I got home and gave Mother the money for the dozen eggs, she quickly counted the money to make certain it was all there. She told me what Dad had said and asked where the money had come from for my ice cream cone. I had to do some fast thinking without technically' lying, and I said, "There were thirteen eggs in the bag, and I thought it would be okay to buy an ice cream cone with the extra money." Mother sternly stated, "Next time, bring all the egg money home."

I must confess at other times (not too often), I would "accidently" miscount and end up with an extra egg in the bag again. Then being very careful to look up and down the road, just to make certain Dad was nowhere in sight, I would rear back on another strawberry ice cream cone! Every penny had to be accounted for. Money was getting scarcer with Dad working less and less in the mines.

The cotton crops began to fail in the early 1940s. By 1943, Dad had determined it was no longer practical to try to grow cotton, due to the bow weevil invasion. He continued to grow corn for the chickens, turkeys, and horse. In the late 1940s, there were severe droughts in the region. We would plant the corn in early May, and it would spring up looking very promising that we would have a good crop. By July, however, the spring rains would cease and the 90 plus degree temperature and the hot sun would be very damaging to the young corn. The corn foliage would twist up and began to turn brown at its base. Sometimes in the late evening, we could hear thunder off in the distance. We hoped it would bring rain but only be disappointed as the clouds dissipated without a trace of rain. Slowly the corn would stop growing. It would try to produce corn but only small nubbin ears about four inches long would be all it would produce. Not nearly enough to feed the animals over winter!

Dad would become very discouraged. Almost daily, he would walk out into the corn looking at the small, twisted stalks and wonder just how many more days it could tolerate the drought before there would be a total crop failure. He studied the skies morning and night hopeful of detecting signs of rain. Mother would fret and worry and ask, "What are we going to do?" Sometimes Dad would say, "I think I'm going to go up to Tennessee or Kentucky and get a job. They say the mines up there are hiring workers and the seams of coal are four to five feet thick!" Mother would chide him about this statement. She knew Dad had passed his prime for working in the mines, and it would be foolish to try and move and start all over again. Dad began to grow strawberries. The strawberries were more drought resistant than other crops and were very much in demand by the local small town folks. They could be sold for about $ 1.50 per gallon. Down in the valleys where the coal had been strip mined, the wild blackberries grew in abundance. Apparently something in the mine slag was very conducive for wild berries to flourish. Dad could pick about five gallons of blackberries per day. Of course, I could never out pick him. Usually between the two of us, we could pick approximately eight gallons per day. These berries could be easily sold in town, and most of the time, there were customers asking for more.

One day Frankie was over at our house playing with me. I had just gathered the eggs and had them in a pail. I told Frankie I had discovered a gigantic strawberry out in the field, and within another day or two it would be fully ripe, and I was going to eat it! Frankie wanted to see this prized strawberry, so I took him out in the patch to show him. As he looked at the huge berry, he reached down as if he was going to pick my berry. I warned him, "You better not pick that berry!" Frankie smiled, then quickly reached down and picked the berry and popped it in his mouth! I was very upset and charged at Frankie, fully intending on giving him a good pounding. He turned and started running, and I couldn't catch him because I was still carrying the bucket of eggs. Still very angry, I took one of the eggs out of the bucket and fired it at Frankie. It hit him square in the back of his head. He stopped cold, the egg was slowly oozing down his neck and shirtless back. He began to cry and shouted, "I'm going to tell your Mother!" I knew Mother would be angry, not so much for hitting Frankie in the head with the egg, but rather for wasting a good egg! I regretted it as well, not so much for hitting Frankie with the egg, but regretting the fact that I could have reared back with another ice cream cone had I not wasted that egg!

I picked up some dry straw from the strawberry patch and wiped the egg off Frankie's head and back. He agreed not to tell Mother. I thought about what Frankie had done. I felt betrayed by my friend. The Bible says, "If you can't be trusted with small matters, then how can you be trusted with major matters?" Could I not trust Frankie? Did Frankie not value our friendship? Did he not respect my request to not eat my prized strawberry? But then I thought, it was only a strawberry, why such a big deal? After all we were standing in a whole big field of ripe strawberries! I wondered what prompted me to become so aggressive. Why did I become so hostile and angry? I didn't understand the changes going on in my body. Preadolescence hormones were changing my behavior.

Each morning as the sun began to rise over Dellah's cornfield, I would sit on the front porch and look over the withering cornfield. The light dew that had settled on the corn during the night would began to vaporize, sending wiggly heat waves up from the cornfield and dissipating into the searing heat of the rising sun. I would pray. "Please, God, please send us some rain before it's too late to save the crops." After about five weeks of scorching heat and no rain, Dad would instruct me to start chopping down the withered corn while there was still some food value in it for the animals. Each day, I would chop down a large bundle of corn and feed it to the cow, hogs, and horse. While the stalks still had some green in them, all the animals would eat it, stalk and all. I had to drag the large bundles of corn quite a distance from the fields to the pig pen and cow and horse stalls.

One day, I thought I might use ole Dolly to help me drag the corn to the animals. I put the bridle on her, and bringing a long rope with me, I rode her to the corn field where I chopped down a large bundle of corn. After getting it cut and tightly bundled up with the rope, I then tied the other end of the rope around my waist. I crawled up on Dolly. It looked like I had come up with a great idea that would save me a lot of hard work. Once securely set on the back of the horse, I told Dolly to get up. She started moving but as soon as the slack had gotten out of the rope and the big bundle of corn began to move behind her, she became frightened and began to run. The faster she ran, the more frightened she became of this big bundle of corn chasing her! By now the rope was cutting into my belly, producing some nasty rope burns. I was holding on for dear life. I pulled back very hard on the reins and at the same time I tried to talk calmly to Dolly, "Whoa, girl, easy girl, steady girl."

Dolly finally stopped running but was still very nervous and kept prancing around. Now she had gotten the rope wrapped around one of her hind legs. While still having the rope tied around my waist and now twisted around Dolly's hind leg, I knew I would probably be trampled to death if I fell off and Dolly panicked again. Finally she calmed down and stood still, and I quickly untied the rope from around my waist and slid down off Dolly. I thought, "That was a pretty stupid idea!" I was very glad ole Dolly could be trusted to never tell Mother what I had done.

Sometimes in the late evening, heavy dark clouds would appear in the Western sky. Although we desperately needed rain, these dark clouds would worry Mother. She was very much afraid of storms and the possibility of a tornado. She had insisted that Dad build a storm shelter. The storm shelter was built about two hundred feet away from the house, which usually meant we would be soaked to the skin before we could reach the shelter. The shelter was dug out into the side of the hill near the pathway down through the pasture to town. It was below ground level, and Dad had covered it with timbers, then tar paper, and finally about a foot deep layer of dirt. It was definitely a safe place to be during severe storms. Due to Mother's fear of storms, we spent much time in that storm shelter. Many times Mother would arouse us late at night and take us to the storm shelter, especially if the wind picked up and there was a lot of lightning and thunder.

One night, we were awakened by Mother just past midnight. Dad grabbed the kerosene lantern from the back porch, and in the wind and pouring rain, we were all herded to the storm shelter. Just before leaving the house, I spied two comic books lying on the dining room table. I grabbed these books and tucked them under my coat to keep them from getting wet. Once in the storm shelter, Mother was nervous and crying in fear of the storm. Dad was holding the door slightly open so he could peek out and assess the severity of the storm. He had placed the lighted lantern on the bench inside the shelter. I pulled out the comic books and handed one to Fred. We huddled around the lantern and began reading the comic books. Mother, still in a panic and crying, saw us reading the comic books and exclaimed. "Our house is being blown away and all you two are interested in is reading those blooming comic books!" (The house didn't blow away!) Sometimes if Delmar Atkins had adequate warning, she would also bring her children up to our house and join us in the storm shelter during a bad storm. The storms were very often quite severe but passed over quickly. If there was any rain at all, it would be a very hard ten-minute downpour which was not adequate at all to break the drought.

One day, a man drove up in a truck and stated he understood we had some piglets for sale. I told him we did have some for sale and took him around to the pig pen to look at them. The ole sow was in the pen but the little piglets could still easily slip through the hog wire and they were nowhere in sight. Most of the time if you called them, they would come running, thinking you were going to feed them. I called, "Pig-ee, pig- ee!" But they failed to come. Apparently they were too far away in the forest to hear as they searched for acorns, mushrooms, or tender roots they could eat. The man began to become impatient and was about to leave. Suddenly I heard the piglets squealing as if being chased. Looking out in the pasture, I saw ole Mickey herding the piglets home! From that day forward, anytime we wanted the piglets, we would simply say, "Mickey, go get the pigs." And in short order, he would go find them and bring them squealing and running (as fast as a little piglet could run) back to the pig pen.

I wondered if ole Mickey would also help me catch a chicken when Mother would ask me to catch one for her to kill for our meal. The chickens were very difficult to catch, and when I tried to catch one, they would always run up under the house. Amazingly, ole Mickey learned very quickly what I wanted him to do. I would point to a chicken and tell Mickey to get that chicken, and he would chase it down and hold it between his front paws until I could get there to take it. The chickens were no longer safe when they retreated up under the house! One night after going to bed, I heard ole Mickey barking off in the woods. He continued to bark for a long while. Since I couldn't go to sleep with all that barking, I got out of bed and took the kerosene lantern and went down in the woods where Mickey was still barking. He had a possum treed in a small tree. I shook the possum from the small tree, and it fell to the ground and played dead or, as the ridge children called it, played possum.

I took the possum by the tail and brought it back home. I placed it under a wash tub and left it on one of the large flat rocks we used as a sidewalk. I placed a large rock on top of the wash tub to keep the possum from being able to escape. The next morning I placed the possum in a burlap sack and took it to the Negro quarters on the western end of the small town. There was a restaurant in this settlement which was used exclusively by the Negroes. They called the restaurant the Blue Moon Cafe. I asked the restaurant owner if she wanted to buy a possum. She asked, "How much?" I stated, "Fifty cents." She stated, "That bees too much fo dat possum, I's give yo a quarter!" I told her she could have it for a quarter.

Unfortunately ole Mickey must have thought he had done well by treeing that possum. From that time forward, he would go off in the woods two or three times a week and tree more possums. He wouldn't stop barking until I got out of bed and would go down and shake the possum from the tree. Fortunately, the lady at the Blue Moon Cafe was always happy to take all the possums I could supply for a quarter each! She told me, "Sweet potatoes and baked possum sho bees good!"

One day in 1947, I had just finished my lunch and went out on the front porch to rest a while. It was almost noon and time for ole No. 12 to come through town. Suddenly, the silence was shattered by the loud air horn of a diesel locomotive as it bore down on the small town. It was the first diesel locomotive I had ever heard. Instead of the usual chug,

chug, chug of the steam engine, the diesel produced a loud constant roar like a very strong wind blowing through the pine trees. I ran from the porch out into the front yard and looked intently toward town hoping to get a glimpse of this new train. I could only faintly see the bright yellow and black locomotive as it sped through the small town. No need to stop; there was no need to take on more water or coal. It didn't even slow down. Fortunately there was not a horse and wagon trying to cross the tracks at that time; they wouldn't have stood a chance against this speeding monster!

Within a very short time, perhaps a month or so, all the steam locomotives had been replaced with the new diesel engines. These old retired steam engines were all now bound for the scrapyards. After years of faithful service, this ending seemed so inappropriate, but that's progress! Now there was no longer a need to supply the railroads with locally mined coal. I missed the steam locomotives with their shrill steam whistles and the hissing sound of the escaping steam. I had often stopped along the railroad tracks to watch the small switch engines at work as I carried the milk to Ma Rosie. There was a side railroad track along the main line running parallel with the small town. Here the switch engine would travel the spur lines from the various mine locations, collecting the coal cars filled with coal and the flat bed pulp wood cars which then would all be hooked together for the larger locomotives to pull them to their northern destinations. The little switch engine would take each individual coal car across a scale to be weighed and then give it a gentle push down the side track to connect its coupler to the awaiting string of cars. The switch engine would give the individual car a shove and then the brakes would be applied to the switch engine, allowing the single coal car to coast down the track to connect with the other cars previously weighed.

I began placing small sticks on the railroad track and watched as the massive steel wheels on the fully loaded coal cars pulverized and crushed them into dust. Each trip, I would select bigger and bigger sticks to place on the tracks. The heavy cars seemed to crush them all very easily. One day, I found a stick about the size of a baseball bat and decided to see if the train would crush a stick this large. The brakeman on the switch engine saw me place the large stick on the track and began yelling at me. I took off running as fast as I could while still carrying the gallon of milk. I think the brakeman got the coal car stopped before it hit the big stick on the tracks. I decided I had better not place anymore sticks on the railroad track. I'm glad I didn't derail that train! Like the bigger steam engines which we had used as clocks to remind us of the time, these smaller switch engines disappeared as well. They were no longer needed to assemble the coal cars together for their trip north. The spur lines became overgrown with tall weeds and brush. Trees which had fallen on the tracks were left to rot away. Everything seemed to be changing.

Just south of the railroad approximately two hundred yards, a prominent small-town businessman named Barney Karr had a very nice barn with a three-acre corral where he kept about twenty to thirty mules and horses. He was a horse trader as well as formerly owning the cotton gin before it closed a few years earlier. His son, Bruce Karr, was in my class throughout all twelve years of schooling. We were fairly good friends and chummed around a lot while in school. I think he also had a crush on Lois. Barney Karr was the first man I remember who bought a large new tractor. It was a big red International Harvester. He hired a man to drive the tractor and contracted it out to other farmers to do their spring turning. Very soon, additional tractors began to appear. I thought how much easier it would be on Dad if we could afford a tractor and then sit in the tractor seat instead of having to walk behind ole Dolly all day. It was only a dream. Tractors were very expensive.

One day, as I walked by the Karr's barn and corral, I noticed there were no horses or mules. The corral was empty. The new tractors were making the horses and mules obsolete. Those unfortunate animals had apparently been shipped off to a slaughter house. Europeans had acquired an appetite for horse meat during the war years. Now all the horses and mules were being slaughtered, then canned and shipped to Europe for consumption by humans. Before the tractors arrived, the mules and horses were a farmer's most prized possession. A farmer valued his horses and took great effort to be certain they were well cared for. How quickly that changed!

As I grew older, in about the fourth grade, I began to develop friendships with other city boys. Bruce Karr, Sonny Christian, Jimmy Sides, and Joe Bowden became good school buddies. None of them, however, came over to the ridge to visit, except Sonny Christian. I never visited in their city homes either. The friendship seemed to exist only in the school environment and did not extend beyond school time or weekends.

Sonny Christian's dad died when he was in the third grade. I remember the day they came and took him out of our classroom due to his father's sudden death. After his father's death, Sonny began coming over to our house on the ridge unannounced several times a week. I think he came for the good country meals Mother cooked. He would usually announce that it would be okay for him to spend the night. Fred, Sonny, and I would all sleep in the same bed. Finally, Mother told me to tell Sonny that he shouldn't come over unless invited. Mother said he ate too much! I wondered if, even though he was a city boy, he really didn't have many good meals at home since his mother was a widow.

Sonny didn't seem to be class conscious. At times it was difficult to socialize with these other city boys. I was old enough now to begin feeling self-conscious about my patched jeans and faded shirts. Mother was either a poor seamstress or just didn't have time to do a good job of patching and sewing rips and tears in my jeans. The patches stood out like a mule in a horse show. The stitching was very large and not neatly sewn. The new patch did not blend well with the older, faded material in the original jeans. I was embarrassed to have to wear these patched pants to school. Sonny seemed not to mind the patched jeans, and I felt his friendship was genuine. We remained good friends throughout our twelve years of schooling.

Since the drought continued and the corn crops failed year after year, Dad decided we should sell the cow and just purchase our milk from the store. He said we could get $150 or more for the cow, and we desperately needed the money, and we couldn't afford to buy feed for the cow anyway. Dad continued to struggle with his failing health. He sold a two-acre parcel of land to a railroad retiree who planned to build his retirement home on the ridge. He debated about whether he should sell ole Dolly. The corn production was so low that it was inadequate to supply the feed necessary to feed the animals over winter. I dreaded the thought of ole Dolly being sent to the slaughter house. I told Dad the next year might be better, and I would be old enough that I would be able to do most of the plowing. Dolly was spared for another year.

I was in the fourth grade and Jody was in the second. I was small for my age and Jody was taller than me and quite a bit heavier. As elementary children usually do, while waiting to be picked up by the school bus after school, they would all line up in a row waiting for the bus. One day I noticed Jody not in line and crying. I asked him what was wrong and he stated a big bully from the fifth grade had pushed him out of line and knocked him down. The next day the bully again gave a big two-handed shove to Jody's chest, knocking him down once again. I saw this and told the bully to stop pushing Jody.

The bully responded, "Oh yea, you want some of this too?" I knew what was coming next and braced myself. He gave me a big two-handed shove in my chest. To his surprise, I didn't even budge. My heavy duty farm chores like carrying in 60 pounds of coal every day had built up some muscles! Before he could attempt another of his two handed shoves, I grabbed him in a big bear hug, lifted his feet off the ground, and slammed him down very hard on the ground. No more bullying from that wimpy kid!

Several months later, I went over to Kip's house to play. Jody was already there. Kip was always an agitator and he said, "Hey, Jody, didn't you tell me last week that you could take Louis in a wrestling match?"

Jody looked embarrassed and had a sheepish grin on his face. He didn't say anything.

Kip goaded him again. "You told me you could take Louis in a fight any day."

I looked at Jody and asked, "Did you say that?" Jody continued to only grin and look down at the ground. I asked if he wanted to wrestle. He said okay. I grabbed Jody in a big bear hug, lifted him off the ground, and slammed him down hard on the ground. While Jody was struggling to get up, I turned to Kip and asked, "Do you want to wrestle to?"

Kip said, "No way!" I turned and went home. I was very disappointed in my two friends. I felt my friendship had been betrayed by Jody and Kip. Should I reevaluate our friendship? Why were these things happening? Why couldn't things remain the same and not change? I was perplexed by my disappointment and anger with my playmates. Subtle changes were taking place in my body, changing me from a gentle child to a more aggressive preadolescent boy!

Racial tension still simmered very heavily in the small town. It didn't take much to provoke a fight. One time, as Fred, Billy Files, Kip Files, and myself were coming home from the small town, I picked up two or three rocks about the size of baseballs to drop off the bridge into the water below. I usually did that every time we walked across the bridge back home. The water was about twenty feet below the bridge, and it made a big splash when the rocks hit the water. When we reached about the middle of the bridge, I let the rocks go.

Suddenly, from under the bridge, I heard someone say, "Who dat chunking? Who dat up der chunking?" Then out from under the bridge came about eight or ten teenage Negro boys and girls. They waded into us, throwing punches, and one of the girls grabbed Kip by his arm and began dragging him away. Kip was only about nine years old. Billy shoved the girl away and grabbed Kip by his arm and started running toward the gate which led to the pathway through the cow pasture. The gate was designed in a Z-shape so people could easily pass through, but the cow couldn't negotiate through it. We all made it through the gate, but the Negros continued to chase us. Being on higher ground, we began throwing rocks at them, and they began throwing rocks back at us. Kip and I started gathering up the rocks and kept Billy and Fred supplied with ammunition. The battle continued for some time, and being outnumbered, we kept retreating up the pathway.

In an attempt to scare the Negros, Fred yelled, "Go get the shotgun, Louis!" One of the older Negro boys seemed to be the leader. He would yell, "Charge!" and they would all rush toward us, throwing a barrage of rocks. Fred and Billy would furiously return the hail of rocks toward them and then their leader would yell, "Fall back, fall back," and they would retreat back down the hill a little way.

It just so happened that the day before, we were playing with an old shotgun on the back porch. It was disabled and could not be fired. It was in three pieces. Remembering this old gun and Fred's yelling for me to go get the gun, I took off running as fast as I could up the pathway to our house. It was only about two hundred yards away. The old shotgun was still on the back porch. I grabbed the three pieces of the gun and ran back down the hill as fast as I could. The rock fight was still going strong.

As I came near the battlefield, I was concealed by a small berm on the hill. I crouched behind the berm and when the Negro leader yelled, "Charge!" and they charged up the hill, I waited until they were about thirty feet away. Then I was holding the gun as if it were fully assembled and functional, and I stood up and aimed the gun squarely at the chest of their leader. He froze in his tracks, then yelled, "They've got a gun! Run, run, run!"

They all ran back across the bridge and kept running as they crouched in the ditches along the road back toward town. Right or wrong, I'm uncertain as to how this battle would have ended were it not for that old gun. I did not intentionally drop the rocks at them under the bridge. I had no idea they were under the bridge until they came out yelling and swinging their fist. Both Fred and Billy had some nice bruises on their chest the next day. I developed a fear of Negroes. Why were they so quick to attack us? Why did I have to be so careful to avoid them in the small town? Why did they hate me?

A few days after the rock fight, I went up to the McDonalds to play with Henry. I was very surprised when Henry told me they were moving to California. Apparently Aunt Mary and Dad's sister, Nell, who lived in California, had written the McDonalds and informed them that John could get a good-paying job in California. She had encouraged them to move. Ma Elliott had lived with the McDonalds until she died in 1947, and now the McDonald clan decided they might find a better life in California. They took a train to California. Their daughter, Alma, was the same age as Lois and I. Henry was about two years younger. There wasn't much time to say good-bye. Within a few days after they had informed us about their plans, they were gone. The old log home stood empty until the land was bought and turned into a cattle ranch. It was then torn down because it interfered with the big tractor which was brought over to maintain the pasture land. My cousins, whom I'd known and played with all my life, had moved away. Perhaps I would never see them again. California was a very long ways away. My friend Jody had also moved. One of the city boys, Jimmy Sides, had also moved. His father had owned the Sides Furniture Store on the main street of the small town for many years. Now the store was shuttered and closed and they had moved away.

The mountain where we lived seemed to be in transformation. It didn't feel the same. The drought had taken its toll on the land. Wilted crops and brown dead grass cast an ugly, lifeless shadow across the landscape. Was I becoming cynical? Were there better places to live? What did the future hold?

When Ma Elliott died, they brought her body back to the old log home. She was placed in the front room for about five days. It would take about five days for all the kin folks to arrive from Florida, California, and Texas. Out of respect for the dead, someone sat by the casket day and night until the day of the funeral. Grandma Elliott was lain to rest alongside her husband in the small town cemetery. At least now she didn't have to worry about having to move to California, Kentucky, or Tennessee.

Cold War (Continuation)

After World War II ended, the hope for world peace ceased almost immediately with the beginning of the Cold War. Being only eleven years old, I couldn't understand how Russia and China went from being our allies during the war to becoming our distrusted enemies in two short years. It affected the lifestyle of everyone in America due to the dreaded threat of atomic warfare. School-aged children as well as adults lived in fear of the possibility of an atomic bomb attack. I recall having a dream one night where the Russians crashed through our back door with their bayonets affixed to their long rifles and proceeded to stab us all to death while we were all in our beds! I worried about the fact that Russia and China had us grossly outmanned. We were outnumbered by about twenty to one. How could we survive an attack? The schools began practicing air-raid drills. Once a month, we would all be herded down to the lowest level of the school building. We would be lined up along the inner walls of the hallways and have to sit with our hands over our heads (not much protection, I thought, from a nuclear attack).

In spite of the threat of nuclear war, life had to go on. Dad determined he couldn't turn the fields anymore for the spring planting due to his crippled legs. His arthritic knees and hip joints could not tolerate all the walking that would be required to turn the land with ole Dolly. He hired Barney Karr's tractor to turn the land and get it ready for planting the corn. I don't know how Dad came up with the money to hire the plowing since it cost twenty dollars per hour for the tractor and operator. I was very impressed as I watched the big red tractor turn over about eight feet of dirt per pass. Within four hours, he had prepared more land for planting than we could do in a week with the horse. It saved Dad a lot of time. I just hoped this year there would be sufficient rain so we would have an abundant crop of corn.

In the summer months, Mother's youngest sister, Thelma, would bring her only child, a daughter named Willie Lee, about one and a half years younger than Lois and I, up to the farm to stay with us for about two weeks. In exchange, Lois and I would be invited to Aunt Thelma and Uncle Ronald's home over in Birmingham for a week. They lived in the area where all the iron and steel mills were located. I didn't really like to go down there. It was smelly and dirty. They lived in the steel mill company's row houses, and there was always a brownish colored cloud from the steel mills suspended in the air. The homes were built identically on the outside. They were built in rows along a long street. The reddish-brown smog from the steel mills settled on everything. All the cars the workers owned who lived in these row houses had the paint peeling off their roofs!

I liked the idea of going to Birmingham on vacation so I could boast about it to the other ridge children. Very few of them ever got to go anywhere beyond the small town. Once there, however, within a few days I was ready to come home. The front yard of Aunt Thelma and Uncle Ronald's house was completely void of any vegetation; no grass and no shrubs, just bare, dirty reddish brown dirt. Once while there, being very bored, I decided to sod their front yard. In the alley behind their house was a very healthy stand of Bermuda grass. I don't know why the grass grew so well in the middle of the alley roadway, but it was thriving very well there. I used a shovel and dug the Bermuda grass up in big clumps. Lois, Willie, and I carried the clumps of grass to the front yard and sodded their yard. It looked nice when we had finished in three or four days, but I don't know if it survived or not in that very acid soil.

When Willie came to the farm for her vacation, she thoroughly enjoyed it. She loved the outdoors, the woods, and especially all the farm animals. Baby chicks, little piglets, or newborn kittens in the barn were all loved by Willie. Although ostensibly there to visit with Lois, most of Willie's time was spent bugging me to do things outside. One of her favorite things to do was persuade me to put the bridle on ole Dolly so she could ride the horse. Willie would sit on that horse for hours while allowing Dolly to graze on the grass along the lane to our house. While being very tomboyish and loving the outdoors, Willie was also very much a beautiful young lady. In 1958, she was selected as Miss Alabama and went on to be selected as first runner-up in the Miss America Beauty Pageant that year. In addition to Willie being an avid outdoorsy type, she was a very talented singer and dancer. After the 1958 beauty pageant, Willie left for Hollywood. I only saw her one other time about 50 years later. She rarely returned to Alabama and never back to the farm.

Sometimes I would think about Willie and wondered if she was happy in Hollywood. Was the glamor and glitter of Hollywood more fun than the time spent as a young lady on the farm? Many young adults were making enormous changes in their lifestyle.

Somehow, in my heart, I never thought Hollywood was a good fit for Willie. I wondered if she ever longed for the good times spent on the farm playing with all the baby animals and riding ole Dolly. Then again, she must be very happy in Hollywood because she spends almost all her time there.

In about 1948, there was a great deal of hype on the radio about an upcoming boxing match for the heavy weight title of the world. I think it was between Joe Lewis and Billy Kohn. We all huddled around the radio and listened intently to the blow-by-blow description of the fight as the radio announcer very vividly gave an exciting minute-by-minute accounting of the fight. Naturally, Joe Lewis won again.

A few days after the big fight, I went over to Frankie's to play. Since the fight was still fresh on our minds, we decided we would have a boxing match in their empty corn crib that was just about the size of a boxing ring. Frankie and his brother, Terry, were going to box and I was going to referee. After flailing wild punches at one another for several minutes, Frankie landed a good punch square on the chin of Terry. Terry crumpled to the floor, obviously knocked out. He lay motionless on the floor for about thirty seconds. Frankie began to scream, "I've killed my brother! I've killed my brother!"

I bent down and shook Terry. I called his name, "Terry? Terry?" Terry popped awake and looked very puzzled about all the commotion. He couldn't understand why all the fuss. I don't think Terry ever realized what had happened.

We talked about this new thing called television. People were saying that one day you would be able to watch boxing matches, movies, and much more right in your own home.

We found this to be unbelievable. How could they send movies through the air right into your own home? That had to be just science fiction! Even the movie theater was still very much a novelty. Every Saturday afternoon, the Pastime Theater in the small town would feature Western-style movies. The cost was ten cents. We loved to go whenever we could afford the admission cost. Some folks in town would tell a story about when the theater first opened, a simple-minded fellow went in the theater for his first Western movie. When the good guys were surrounded by the Indians, this simple-minded fellow pulled out his pistol and shot the movie screen full of holes! Now they're talking about movies being viewed in a big box right in your own living room. It really wasn't just science fiction!

James had just graduated from Auburn University and had taken a teaching job in Birmingham. One weekend, he came up to the farm and took me back to Birmingham with him. One evening, after dark, James took me downtown to the big shopping district of Birmingham. There I saw my very first television. One of the big department stores had three televisions on display in their window. I was amazed; it was just like being at the Pastime Theater except you could buy this astonishing new thing called television and watch it in your home.

In late 1949 or 1950, Kate and Oscar Meyers bought a television set. The United States provided a ten thousand dollar death benefit policy on all the soldiers during World War II. After Dugan was killed, eventually Kate and Oscar received this insurance money and used some of it to buy a television. The Meyers television was the very first television brought to the ridge. It presented a problem, however, for Kate and Oscar. Their visitors were never-ending. All the ridge families were dying to see this amazing invention.

Finally Aunt Kate had to establish some rules. All the children and adults could come over on Thursday and Friday evenings from 6:00 to 9:00 pm. Other times would be only if invited.

Kate and Oscar's house was always crowded on Thursdays and Fridays, and you had to get there early in order to get a good seat. Kate was very generous about inviting the children many other times when there was a program she knew they would enjoy. After about five or six years, the price for a television was much more reasonable and many rural homes began buying them. You could always tell who had recently purchased a television due to the shiny new mast and antenna mounted alongside the still very primitive rural homes. Soon after, televisions began appearing in rural America, the telephone companies began installing telephone cables as well. Everyone now needed a television and a telephone in their home (not yet indoor plumbing or bathrooms, but that could wait.)

The first year Dad had the big red tractor turn the ground in the spring, we had a fairly good corn crop. Fred and I now did most of the plowing. Mother didn't want Fred to get too hot or too tired, so we traded off with the plowing very frequently (unfair for ole Dolly, she didn't get many rest periods). We all weeded the corn. Even Mother would help us in the early morning. Sometimes our corn weeding would have to wait if Dellah or Jim Delevechio wanted us to work in their fields. Once the corn was harvested that fall, there was ample corn to get us through the winter. I was very thankful for the good harvest. Now ole Dolly would have food for the winter months, and Dad wouldn't consider selling her.

One Friday afternoon on the way home on the school bus, Fred challenged the Bynum Camp boys to a game of football on Sunday afternoon. They accepted the challenge and the time was set for 3:00 p.m. in the plowed field out in front of Ma Files's house. At 3:00 p.m. Sunday, Fred, Billy Files, Jerry Files, and me were ready to proudly represent the ridge community against Roger Estell, Charles Estell, Charles Thornbro, and Billy Joe Nickelson from Bynum Camp. We won the toss, and the Bynum Camp boys kicked off to us. It was full speed, full contact tackle football. There were no helmets and no pads. After six or eight plays, we were able to run the ball in for a score. Fred then kicked off to the Bynum Camp boys. Charles Thornbro caught the kick and immediately began to streak down my side of the field.

Charles was a fifteen year old and a fairly good sized boy. I was about twelve years old and weighed only seventy pounds. As Charles lumbered toward me, I thought I had better tackle him low around the ankles, or he would just run right over me and score a touchdown. I closed my eyes and dived for his ankles. I locked my arms around his big feet and squeezed as tightly as I could. His feet stopped so suddenly it was like they had been instantly nailed to the ground. Charles fell very hard, head first, onto the plowed field. He had the breath knocked out of him; his lip was bleeding and his mouth was full of dirt. He struggled to get his wind back. He spit some blood from his mouth and stated "I quit!" Then all the Bynum Camp boys headed back home. Meanwhile, I was hearing bells and seeing stars. Everything seemed to be in a fog and my legs wouldn't support me. Still groggy, Jerry Files lifted me up in the air, and our whole team began slapping me on the back and shouting. Jerry said, "You hit him like an atom bomb. That's what we're going to call you. Little Atom." That name stuck for a couple of weeks but then was discontinued.

I was very glad. I didn't like that name. I don't know if Charles admired me for my grit or my stupidity, but Charles began to come around and hang out with me. Personally, if I could do it all over again, I think I would just step aside and let Charles lumber right on by. Charles was very shy at the time, and I suspected, like many other boys, he had a crush on Lois but was too shy to talk directly with her. Charles would come up on the ridge two or three times a week, and we would just hang out. If it were baseball season, he would come up to visit with a new baseball and play catch. The next time up, he would bring a new glove. When he would leave to go home, he would say, "You can have the ball and glove. I won't use them anymore unless I come up here."

He was the most generous, nurturing young man one could ever imagine. Usually when he came to visit, he would bring pop, chips, or candy to share. Sometimes he would bring a package of hot dogs and buns, and we would build a fire in the woods and roast them. One time he brought a whole chicken, and we tried to roast it over a fire in the woods. It was after dark when we thought it was ready to eat. I'm sure we ate a very burnt chicken which was still raw inside. Being almost four years older than me and much stronger, Charles favorite trick was to grab my arm and twist it behind my back until it was quite painful (perhaps this was payback for that shoestring tackle.)

Charles had, however, an ingrown toenail on his big toe. This was very painful and sore. When he would twist my arm, I would retaliate by stomping on that big toe. He would immediately let go of my arm and grab that big toe, clutching it and moaning in pain. I owned Charles due to that sore toe. Such a strange relationship; but a most amazing and lasting friendship!

One who has unreliable friends soon comes to ruin. But there is a friend who sticks closer than a brother. (Proverbs 18:24)

In the spring of 1949, Dad again hired a tractor to prepare the ground for planting. Mr. Pierce came over with a much smaller Ford Tractor. Observing the tractor, I felt it wasn't big enough to do a good job of turning the dirt. It, however, proved me wrong. It pulled the turning disc with ease, and at the end of each pass, the operator would use the newly developed hydraulic lift, which permitted him to turn much more quickly and easily in close quarters. It was even faster than the big red International Harvester tractor. Fred and I would use ole Dolly and a log to drag the ground smooth and make a firm seed bed for the corn. Dad would then plant the corn, using the one row corn planter being pulled by ole Dolly. He would start at the edge of the field, about three feet in, and plant the first row of corn. Then, very carefully and skillfully, he would eyeball the three feet distance between each consecutive row. He kept all the rows very uniformly spaced.

If he wanted ole Dolly to move slightly to the right, he would softly say, "Gee, gee," and the horse would respond with a slight move to the right. If more movement to the right was required, then Dad would give a much stronger "Gee, gee!" and Dolly would respond, thereby keeping the rows very straight. Of course, if you needed to move to the left, you gave the command, "Haw." The corn was planted about the end of April, and by the middle of July, it was in full tassel with small pencil-sized ears just beginning to develop.

One morning, we had had a slow steady rain all night long. Dad came into the house out of the rain and exclaimed, "This rain is going to ruin those small nubbin ears of corn!"

I was concerned. What was going to happen? Would that much rain cause the little nubbin ears to mildew or rot or something? I asked Dad, "I thought the rain was good for the corn. How is it going to ruin it?" This was one of the very few times I'd ever heard Dad joke about anything.

He stated, "It's going to make big fat ears out of them!" He laughed and slapped his leg with delight about the prospects of a very good corn harvest that fall. A few days later, another rain storm appeared to be developing on the western horizon. It was late in the evening and a breeze began to pick up.

Mother began to worry about a storm developing. A short while later, the storm was rumbling much closer and the wind was getting stronger. Mother rounded all of us children up and took us to the storm shelter. The storm struck with powerful winds and torrential rain. We remained in the storm shelter until long after dark. Finally, things settled down and we left the storm shelter. As we left the shelter to return to the house, we noticed the ground was covered with large hail stones. We all went to bed and the night was peaceful. The rain had cooled down the hot July air, and I enjoyed sleeping in the now comfortable cool night air.

Early the next morning, before I had gotten out of bed, I heard Mother and Dad talking in the kitchen. It sounded like a very serious conversation. I got out of bed and got dressed. I went into the kitchen and Mother and Dad were both sitting at the kitchen table and both appeared very concerned about something. I looked at them in an inquisitive way as if to say, "What's wrong?" Dad was the first to speak. He stated, "That bad storm last night destroyed our cornfield, it's all blown over and laying on the ground."

My heart sank. We were so happy a few days before about the prospect of a very good corn harvest in the fall.

What terrible news. I quickly went outside to survey the damage. I noticed the pole bean vines in the garden were all twisted and blown over. I then walked over where I could view the cornfield. It was worse than I expected. All the nice tall stalks of corn were now lying flat on the ground. The corn tassels would not be able to pollinate the little ears of corn that had just begun to develop. The hail had shredded the corn leaves. It would no longer be able to process the nutrients from the soil and the sunlight to nurture the small ears and make them grow. I reached down and pulled one of the stalks back up straight. When I let it go, it fell back to the ground.

As I stood there looking over the destroyed cornfield, Dad came up beside me. He looked as if he was going to cry. I'd never seen Dad cry. We stood looking over the destroyed cornfield in silence. Dad then spoke. He said, "I been thinking, now that you've gotten older, maybe we could make some money this summer by cutting timber off the hillside and selling it." My spirits were uplifted. It felt good that Dad appeared to be talking with me as man to man and no longer as a child. He appeared to be asking for my opinion about his suggestion. Timbering on a mountain side is dangerous and hard work. Dad seemed to be asking me if I was up to the task. Was I now capable of doing this hard and dangerous work?

I looked at Dad and said, "When are we going to start?" He stated he would have to go into town and buy a two-man crosscut saw, and we'd be able to begin as soon as he bought the saw. A few days later, we began cutting timber with the newly purchased two-man crosscut saw. There was a 2 day training period. Dad would say, "Stop riding the saw, let the saw do the work, keep the saw level, you're sawing downhill." It was very hot in the woods in the middle of July. Fred's seizures seemed to have worsened. Mother flatly refused to allow Fred to engage in such hot and heavy work. Dad and I cut timber all summer until it was time to start school again. We used ole Dolly to skid the logs up to the top of the hill where they could be loaded onto a truck and transported to Bill Early's Saw Mill, which was located just south of the small town.

By fall we had cut several loads of timber. It was mostly red oak, hickory, and maple. There was a nice grove of pine trees growing along the creek at the bottom of the property. This timber would have been much easier to cut since it was on relatively flat land. Dad said we wouldn't cut those trees this year but maybe save them until next summer. I think he anticipated that by next year, he would not be capable of cutting and skidding the larger hardwood timber off the steep hillside. Hopefully he would still be capable of cutting the pines down by the creek.

That fall, when we harvested the corn, it only produced about one-fourth the amount we had hoped for before the big storm. I don't know if Dad had treated the older boys the same way he was now treating me, but I suspect he did. I was no longer a boy. He consulted with me about the farmwork. He seemed to value my opinion. Once he told me we needed to build a new hen house. The old one was falling down and needed a new roof. We discussed how the new one should be built. He had his ideas and I had mine. After much debate, I expected him to say, "We'll build the hen house just the way I've planned." Instead he said, "All right, we'll build it according to your plans." I now no longer received orders at the supper table for the next day's work. Now we worked as a team. Each respected the other's ideas and suggestions.

As fall approached, Dad said we needed to get in our winter's supply of coal. Generally, while he was working, we would buy three or four tons of coal for our winter's use. Now however, Dad said we would mine our own coal. There was a seam of coal jutting out of the side of the mountain at the base of No. 11 Hill along the small stream. One evening, Dad said the next day we would take some hand tools with us and go down to the coal location and clean off the dirt so we could access the coal. Early the next day we gathered up our tools, shovels, picks, and an auger and long auger drill bit. Dad took a sack and placed in it the necessary material for blasting the coal from the mountain seam. We spent all day cleaning the rock and dirt from around the seam of coal. As we dug deeper, the rock above the coal became more solid and hard, and we could no longer dig it away with just hand tools. Dad had a keg of black powder, in a sealed metal can, which he kept stored up in the loft of the barn. He pulled the contents from the sack he had brought and prepared to make some explosives to blast the coal from the mountain side. I watched as Dad took several sheets of old newspaper and rolled it around a shovel handle. Once about five thicknesses of newspaper were wound tightly around the shovel handle, he took a roll of masking tape and wound the tape around the newspaper so it could not come unwound when removed from the shovel handle. Then he slid the paper off the shovel handle. He stuffed one end of the open cylinder up into the cylinder to form a bottom. Then he poured the black powder into the cylinder until it was full. He packed the black powder firmly into the cylinder and then taped the top closed. He then took an ice pick and punched a hole into the dynamite stick in the middle of the stick. Then he inserted a fuse wire into the hole and taped it in place so it was secure. He cut the fuse about ten feet long. He made two of these dynamite sticks. He pointed out two places along the bottom of the coal seam where he wanted me to use the auger and bit and drill two holes as deep as I could using the bit which was about seven feet long and about two inches in diameter. Once the holes were drilled, Dad took the two sticks of dynamite and shoved them into the freshly drilled holes. He waded up some more paper, and using the shovel handle, he packed the wad of paper firmly in front of the dynamite in the hole. Then he made some very stiff mud from dirt with a little water. The holes were then firmly packed with the mud, making certain the fuse was extended out of the holes about three feet.

Once both holes were prepared for blasting, Dad told me I needed to be at least one hundred feet away from the blast location. I slowly began backing away as I watched Dad light the fuses with a match. I could hear the hissing of the lighted fuses as Dad moved slowly and confidently away from the blasting area. He had done this many times before deep down inside the coal mines he had previously worked in. It took about three minutes before the hot fire on the lighted fuse reached the dynamite at the bottom of the hole. The explosion wasn't as loud as I had expected. Being buried seven feet deep into the coal muffled the noise considerably. I could, however, feel the earth beneath my feet shake from the powerful blast. I had my eyes fixed on the location of the blast area. Huge chunks of coal began to tumble down the mountain side. We then went over to inspect the blast area. Dad stated that when we cleaned it up, we would most likely have a sufficient amount of coal to supply our needs for the winter. He said we would quit for the day, but the next big job would be shoveling the coal into our wagon and hauling it back home. It would require six or seven wagon loads to get all the coal home.

The next day we hitched ole Dolly to the wagon and began hauling the coal home. I felt sorry for ole Dolly; she will have to work very hard pulling all those heavy loads of coal up the steep No. 11 Hill.

Within three days, we had all the coal hauled to the house and dumped it about fifty feet from the back door of our house. It was very hard work mining that coal, but I felt rewarded when I observed the large pile of coal stock piled for our winter's use. Now the whole family would stay warm all winter.

James had left his teaching job in Birmingham after just one year. His temperament wasn't suited for dealing with high school children all day. He took a job in North Alabama near Huntsville as a county agent with the State Department of Agriculture. Very frequently, all the adult siblings and their spouses would come to the farm for the weekend. Many times they would not arrive on Friday night until past midnight. All of us younger children would be rousted out of bed so the older ones could have our beds. We didn't mind; we were very glad to see them and have them visit for the weekend.

On one of his visits home, James talked with Dad about the possibility he might be eligible for disability compensation from the Veteran's Administration. He was aware of the failing health of Dad, and James was himself receiving a partial disability compensation due to his war injury. James encouraged Dad to apply for the disability compensation and suggested he would take a day off work to take Dad down to the Veterans Administration in Birmingham to apply for the compensation. Dad was skeptical; he doubted he would qualify for the disability compensation. James called and made an appointment with the Veteran's Administration. On the day of the appointment, James arrived and took Dad with him to the appointment in Birmingham. This required a lot of paperwork and a physical examination by a Veteran's Administration physician. After the physical and completion of all the paperwork, the Veteran's Administration informed Dad that he should receive the results of their determination within two weeks. Dad still remained skeptical. Little in the way of good fortune had ever come his way. Why build up false hope?

It was now fall and the beginning of a new school year. I was fourteen and now ready for the eighth grade. At the beginning of each new school year, the teacher would give the students a list of required textbooks and other supplies. It was the student's responsibility to acquire his own supplies and textbooks. Once school was over that first day and you arrived back home, you would immediately hop on your bike and pedal as fast as you could to a child's home who was one grade above you in hopes of beating other kids there in order to buy his secondhand books. The going rate was always less than one-half price for the used textbooks. Sometimes you would have to visit three or four older students in order to acquire all the books your teacher had listed. Fred was entering his senior year of school. The first half of the school year, he missed the majority of the time due to his illness. By year's end, however, the seizures had stopped, and Fred was able to attend his classes regularly.

The Veteran's Administration sent Dad a letter in a very official government envelope. Mother anxiously opened the envelope and began to read it for Dad. She began to cry as she read the part which stated, "We have determined that you are eligible for 100 percent disability compensation as a war veteran." As she read further, it stated that Dad's compensation would commence in October and that Dad would receive monthly compensation in the amount of sixty dollars for the remainder of his life. That was more monthly income than we had seen in several years. Most importantly, it would be steady income every month! Mother felt we could get by on that amount each month. What great news that was; now we wouldn't have to fret and worry so much over drought, hail, or floods. There would always be steady monthly income.

One day in the fall of 1949, as I got off the school bus at our bus stop, I noticed a truck with a cattle trailer leaving our house by the lane west of our house. It was about to enter the main road as soon as the school bus passed. I walked up the lane to our house but continued around toward the barn. I assumed Dad would be there, and I could ask him about the visitors. Dad was standing by the barn. I glanced over and saw the horse stall was open and ole Dolly was gone. Dad looked at me and simply said, "I sold the horse."

I think he felt it would be more impersonal to say, "I sold the horse," rather than say, "I sold ole Dolly." A lump came in my throat. I could feel anger welling up inside me. How could he sell ole Dolly? I thought about how hard Dolly had worked all summer, skidding all those logs up the hillside, and how she had pulled all that coal up No. 11 Hill. Dad tried to soften the shock of this news. He stated, "With my disability check now coming in each month, we won't have to farm anymore. If we don't farm, there's no need to feed a horse." I looked at Dad's face; it was obvious this was a difficult decision for him to make but from a practical point of view, it was the correct decision. I'm fourteen now, almost a man, I must learn to deal with these losses. They seem to never end. I told Dad, "I understand. I just hope whoever bought ole Dolly will take good care of her." I didn't ask who bought her or where she was going. But deep inside, I just hoped she wasn't going to the slaughter house. I walked past the barn where all the harnesses for ole Dolly always hung. The harnesses were all still there. My heart sank. Where is she going that there's no need for harnesses? I took a walk up the lane. I thought of all the memories I had of ole Dolly.

How she swam with us at Icy Doe, how gentle she was and allowed us to sit on her back while she grazed in the pasture, and how she would always walk toward you in the pasture when you had her bridle in your hands, willingly opening her mouth to accept the bit you slipped into her mouth. Willing to accept that ole bit, then work at whatever task you had chosen for her to do that day. Now I had to accept the fact I'd never see her again. Why so many losses? Friends had moved, relatives had moved, no more steam engine whistles at night now that the diesel engines roared through town without stopping, and now an empty horse stall and no horse. Sometimes I felt as if I just wanted to leave this ole mountain myself.

Sometimes at school on Fridays, word would go around that there would be a party at the bottom of No. 11 Hill or down by Cranford Creek on the eastern side of the ridge. Older teenage boys would get there first and build a big bonfire. Just at dark, the teenagers would begin to assemble. Mostly they just hung out; the boys in one group and the girls in another. They played a game called go walking. A boy or girl would say, "I make a motion that Doris go walking with Fred." It was like a double dog dare. If the motion was made, you had to go or else face the wrath of being called chicken for the rest of the evening.

Most of the boy's motions to go walking were payback for having nominated a friend to walk with one of the more unattractive girls. The girls took it more seriously and pled with the other girls to make a motion for them to go walking with a boy they really, really liked. Although unsupervised by any adults, these parties seldom got out of hand. After about nine or ten o'clock, the party would began to break up, and the teenagers would start leaving and walking back home. On one occasion, as a group of kids were walking home, I noticed a tenth grade boy holding Lois's hand. She was only fourteen, and I was obligated to watch out after her. Dad had now entrusted me with looking after family affairs. I must keep the family ship shape; it was my responsibility. This boy was not showing respect for my little sister. He had not done the honorable thing by asking Mother or Dad if it would be okay to walk Lois home. When we got to the lane leading up to our house, I intervened. "Okay, you can cut her loose right here." I had to look out for the welfare of our family. My little sister had to be protected. After all, I'm no longer a child; I'm a man just like Dad!

In the early spring of 1950, Fred was almost ready to graduate from high school. Since James now lived in North Alabama, he picked up an application from the Redstone Arsenal in Huntsville for Fred to complete. They were seeking young men interested in applying for apprenticeships in the machine tool trades. Fred completed the application form and returned it to the Arsenal. A quick response was received from the Arsenal, and they offered to hire Fred for an apprenticeship as a machinist. A job would be waiting for Fred as soon as he graduated in May.

As was common for rural kin folks, James invited Fred to come and live with him and his wife, Novis, while he completed the apprenticeship at the Arsenal. By the first of June, Fred would be packing his clothes and moving to Huntsville. Now there would only be Lois and me still living at home.

It was still early April. Fred had been to town, and on his way home, he noticed from the bridge that the creek was full of fish. The fish were red horse suckers, and they were moving up the creek on a spring spawning run. Fred quickly came home and told me to dig some worms so we could go back down to the creek and try to catch these fish. I went out to the moist dirt around the pig pen and quickly dug up some worms. We grabbed some fishing poles and went back down to the creek to fish. We dropped our hooks baited with the worms into the water, but the fish didn't appear interested in the worms. We dropped those worms right in front of a big sucker's nose, but the fish just ignored it. They weren't interested in our worms. No matter how much we tried, not a single bite! Finally, being very frustrated, Fred said, "The only way we're going to get these fish is with a stick of dynamite!"

We went by the Files's house on the way home. We told Jerry and Billy about all the fish in the creek and how they wouldn't bite a hook. There was a serious discussion on how we could catch those fish. Jerry asked, "Do you know where we can get some dynamite?"

I said, "Dad has a whole metal can full of black powder up in the loft of our barn." Jerry then said, "Do you know how to make a stick of dynamite?"

I said, "Sure, when Dad and I mined our coal last fall, I watched how he made the dynamite we used to blast out the coal."

Jerry then said, "You make a stick of dynamite tonight, and after school tomorrow, we will meet at the bridge and dynamite the creek." (If those suckers won't bite a hook, you've gotta get a mess of fish somehow!") I told Jerry we would need a flashlight battery and a long piece of two-stranded electrical wire. He said he could bring that.

That night, I slipped up in the barn loft and made a stick of dynamite just like I had watched Dad make. Since it was to be exploded in the water, we couldn't use a fuse wire. We would need a blasting cap to ignite the dynamite, using electricity from the flashlight battery. I found a blasting cap in the smoke house where Dad kept them.

The next afternoon after school, we all met at the bridge with our supplies to begin our fishing trip. Jerry and Billy showed up with a flashlight battery and about twenty-five feet of two-stranded electrical wire. We decided it might be better to move down the creek away from the bridge. We selected a fairly deep hole where the suckers were abundant. We prepared the dynamite, and I dropped it into the water. It began to float away down the creek. I retrieved it, and using the masking tape, I taped a rock to the dynamite.

I lowered the dynamite into the water again and it sank quickly to the bottom. Fred unwound the electrical wire to its full extension, and we all lay down on our bellies as Fred touched the two pieces of electrical wire to each end of the flashlight battery. There was a muffled swoosh when the dynamite exploded, and a huge geyser of water erupted from the creek. The geyser erupted higher than the trees along the bank. We felt the ground shake! Fred said, "I think you used too much black powder Louis." We stood up to survey the results. There were red horse suckers flopping all over the bank of the creek. Many more were flopping on the surface of the water and some were even suspended from the bushes along the creek. Fred and Billy jumped into the creek and began throwing the fish out onto the bank. Jerry and I gathered all the fish that were scattered all over the woods. We put the fish in a big burlap bag and took them home.

Fresh fish for everyone for several days. I showed the big catch of fish to Dad. I didn't tell him how we had caught them. Dad looked at the fish and stated, "Those fish aren't any good to eat, they're full of tiny bones and unfit to eat." I got a shovel and buried them in the garden. At least they would be good as fertilizer. I don't know who leaked the story about our dynamiting the creek to Dad, but someone didn't keep quiet about it. A few days later he stated, "You got those fish by dynamiting the creek, didn't you?" I thought the next thing to happen would be Dad pulling off his belt and giving me a good whipping. Instead he simply said, "Don't do that again, it's against the law." Dad seemed to recognize that even though I was now a man, sometimes I still behaved like a child and did some foolish things.

Sequel: Cold War (1946 1950)

Right after the ending of World War II in 1945, the Cold War began and lasted for forty-six years. It was almost as stressful as the actual war years themselves. Joseph Stalin, dictator of Russia, harbored strong resentment and hostility against the United States for not coming to his aide more quickly when Germany invaded Russia. Russia lost over twenty million people during the German invasion. The war against China and Russia by Germany began in the late 1930s, and the United States didn't enter the war until 1941. Once the United States entered the war in 1941, the German army was stretched very thin as they now had to fight the war on the Western and Eastern fronts in Europe.

Several skirmishes occurred over the next forty-six years. Russia began annexing and occupying smaller European neighboring countries. Russia expanded her borders into East Poland, Lithuania, East Finland, Romania, and also including the Russian satellite state of East Germany. These rapid invasions by Russia caused great concern for the United States. The United States had hoped to reestablish the European economy and stabilize that part of the world, which had been devastated by the ravages of World War I and

II. In 1949, Communist China was successful in deposing the Nationalist Chinese Government from mainland China to the Island of Formosa. There were continuous skirmishes between Nationalist China and Communist China. The super powers were careful to call these skirmishes *conflicts* and avoided the term *war*.

In 1950, Communist North Korea invaded South Korea. This conflict lasted until 1953. The whole world lived in fear that one of these skirmishes would escalate into all-out atomic war. The United States began building up its military strength. Military spending increased over 400 percent above that utilized during World War II. President Truman authorized the development of the hydrogen bomb, a weapon far more powerful than the atomic bomb, if you can imagine such! By 1949, Russia had already developed their own atomic bomb and were working on a delivery system comprised of intercontinental ballistic missiles. The United States began developing an arsenal of long-range strategic bombers in 1947. These bombers were equipped with nuclear bombs, and a sufficient number of these bombers were always in the air, ready to deliver their payload of atomic bombs anytime the command would have been given by the president of the United States. Russia began to encircle Western Europe with intercontinental- missiles equipped with nuclear warheads. Both the United States and Russia had amassed a stock pile of nuclear weapons capable of totally destroying the world!

In 1948, Russia closed the borders to Western Berlin and declared a blockade by land into the western portion of Berlin occupied by the United States and other western nations. America and other European countries had over half a million military personnel in Berlin when the blockade was imposed. Winston Churchill, in a speech about this blockade and other military closing of borders by Russia, was the first to coin the phrase, "An iron curtain has descended across our continent." In May of 1949, the United States began a massive air lift into Berlin, supplying the blockaded city with needed supplies and military equipment. This air lift, thereby, negated the effects of the blockade imposed by Russia.

The continuous skirmishes during the Cold War between 1947 and 1991 led to a massive buildup of atomic weapons. Missiles were further developed, nuclear submarines were built, the space race began, and clandestine spying and espionage were developed into a science. It brought about movies such as the *James Bond* series. In 1989, the Berlin Wall was dismantled and was a significant step toward stabilizing the German economy.

In 1970, a treaty limiting the proliferation of atomic weapons by the United States and Russia was signed. It wasn't effective, however, in reducing the amount of worldwide tension. Tension continued until the major dismantling of the Soviet Union in 1991.

During the almost fifty years of Cold War posturing by Russia and the United States, the free world was being held hostage by the threat of atomic war. The potential for war to break out anytime caused all the world to live in fear. It wasn't a peaceful or pleasant time to live. From age ten until age fifty-five, my generation of Americans had to endure the imminent fear of weapons of mass destruction. A war which most likely would have destroyed the whole world and every living creature. Ironically, the fear of this atomic bomb itself, thus far, has been the only deterrent which has prevented this unspeakable and catastrophic event from happening!

High School Age

I was finally taller than Lois! Finally, my much anticipated growth spurt had begun. The fine facial fuzz began to thicken and darken. Hair began to grow in strange places on my body, like my arm pits! I had not yet begun to admire the girls my age. Most were still skinny with straight unkempt hair and no makeup. Older girls, however, were a different story. How different they made me feel; pretty faces, shapely bodies, and sexy makeup. Things were changing in my body very quickly. My male hormones had kicked in big time.

One day, Dellah and her daughter came up for a visit with mother. The daughter's name was Bessie May, and she was probably in her early twenties. She was wearing very short red shorts and her blouse was tied in a bow, exposing her well-tanned midriff. Her hair was dark brown and cascaded down to her shoulders in beautiful, long curls. I was spellbound by such beauty. I thought, this must be the most beautiful woman in all the world! Besides that, she smelled good! While sitting in our living room with her shapely legs crossed, she proceeded to pull a pack of cigarettes from her tight shorts and light it with a fancy gold lighter. She blew puffs of smoke while gently tossing her head upward while exhaling the smoke. I'd only seen women like that in magazine pictures. Up until this time my exposure to modern, sexy women had been very limited, or maybe before these changes in my hormones had taken place, I hadn't even noticed. Whatever, I couldn't keep my eyes off her.

Once television became more common, I realized there was another whole different world out there filled with glamorous women. It wasn't just about voluptuous women in sexy clothes that was appealing. Young married women with their soft, smooth skin, gentle voices, and loving devotion to their husbands was very attractive. How fortunate were my older brothers and cousins who had found and married their attractive wives. One day, I hoped I'd find a good wife because I could see how happy these young couples were. That had to wait, however, as I was still too young and didn't have all the resources I needed to woo and charm a woman.

As we rode the bus to school each day, sometimes in the winter the roads would get very muddy and slippery. The school bus would have a difficult time climbing the steep hills. Our bus driver was an older man named Mr. Snow. If the bus tires began to slip and spin in the mud, Mr. Snow would ask all the boys to get off the bus and push it up the hill. He never seemed to recognize that this worked only on our way back home after school. In the morning, as we were headed toward school and Mr. Snow asked us to push the bus, we would, instead of pushing, hold the bus back! He never seemed to figure out why we could always get the bus up the slippery hills in the afternoons but never in the mornings!

In the fall of 1950, Charles Thornbro and another Bynum Camp boy named James Clark and I would plan to go squirrel hunting after we got home from school. Charles should have graduated that year, however, he was held back a year in elementary school. I would get off the bus at our house, then grab a baked sweet potato from the warming oven on the stove and the old shotgun off the wall. I would then walk up to the McDonald's old place and wait for Charles and Clark (we always called him by his last name) to come back up No. 11 Hill with their guns. Then we would walk over to the Swindle's house to get their dog, ole Eisenhower, to go squirrel hunting. Ole Mickey never seemed to get the hang of squirrel hunting. Mickey would tree a squirrel okay, but if the squirrel leaped from tree top to tree top, Mickey would never visually follow it but remain barking up the original tree. Ole Ike, on the other hand, was very skilled at watching the squirrel until it settled in a tree, then he would keep barking until we got there to shoot the squirrel.

Ole Ike was always ready to go squirrel hunting. When we reached the Swindle's house we would call, "Here, Ike. Here, Ike," and ole Ike would come crawling out from under the house. He was a medium-sized dog, mostly white with black spots and very skinny. We would usually bring a biscuit or pieces of scrap meat for Ike to eat when we went hunting. Beyond the Swindle house, there were no more roads or houses, just hills and woods and more hills and woods. Ole Ike would bound off into the woods in search of a squirrel. All we had to do was wait until we heard him barking, then hurry as fast as we could to where he had the squirrel treed.

Unfortunately, ole Ike covered considerable distances in search of a squirrel. Most likely, it would take us fifteen to twenty minutes to negotiate up and down the mountains and valleys to get where ole Ike was treed. We would arrive at the tree and shoot the squirrel. As soon as we did this, ole Ike would be off again in search of another squirrel. We never knew which direction he would take, and we would just wait and listen until we heard him barking again. Most times he would be over a mile away, and we had to listen very carefully to hear the barking from that distance.

He would go north or south or east or west, and by the time we had chased him down four or five times, we would sometimes be totally disoriented in our direction. We'd be lost and darkness was beginning to close in on the woods. We would then climb to the nearest hill and search for familiar landmarks. Cyclone Mountain was to the west, Hickory Ridge was to the east, and Bald Mountain was to the north. From our vantage point on the hilltop, we could then get our orientation back. We would locate and identify the various mountains and then know which way to go in order to get back home. We knew if we headed in the direction of Bald Mountain, it would lead us out of the woods and back home. Squirrel hunting wasn't so much about sport but rather about getting protein for the table. Many folks from the small town as well as almost all the rural folks hunted squirrels and rabbits for food. By the time I was old enough to hunt, squirrels and rabbits were very scarce unless you ventured deep into the woods like we did. When it would begin getting dark, we would head home and ole Ike would just leave us and go back to the Swindle's house.

One afternoon, as we were hunting, ole Ike treed a squirrel some distance away. We went over to where he was barking, not really noticing where we were. We were on Jim Delevicheo's land. As we got to the tree where ole Ike was barking, Jim Delevicheo stepped out from a hiding place with a loaded shotgun. He stated, "I've caught you boys trespassing and now I'm going to take you in." We all had guns and I hoped Charles and Clark wouldn't do anything foolish like aiming their guns back at Jim. I unbreached my gun and ejected the shell, hoping Charles and Clark would do the same thing. I explained to Jim I wasn't aware that we were on his land, and we would get off his land just as quickly as possible. I told him to point the way which would be the quickest for us to get off his land. I also told him there was no way we could call ole Ike off that treed squirrel except by coming down to where he was. Jim talked a few moments about how he didn't want anyone trespassing on his land. Then, surprisingly, he said he would hunt with us for a while. I was very uncomfortable hunting with him after that encounter. After a few minutes, I told Charles and Clark I was ready to quit hunting and go home. When I got home, I told Dad what had happened. I assumed Jim would complain to Dad about me hunting on his property. I don't think he ever did or at least Dad never mentioned it to me if he did.

On another squirrel hunting episode, we were walking down the lane to the Swindle's house to get ole Ike. Charles and Clark both had shotguns, but I only had our single-shot .22-caliber rifle. We heard a flock of crows cawing a short distance away. Being aware that I could call the crows and they would come swooping over, Charles asked me to call them so we could shoot at them. I stated, "I'll call them but you two will have to let me shoot first, since I only have my single shot .22 rifle and you two have shotguns." They agreed they wouldn't shoot until after I did.

I began calling and the flock of crows came swooping in right away. We were hiding in a thicket of pine trees. As the crows got directly over us, I aimed and fired my rifle. A crow came tumbling out of the sky and fell right at our feet. I thought either Charles or Clark had shot it with their shotguns. It would have been an amazing shot for me to have hit a flying crow with my .22 rifle.

Charles asked Clark if he had shot. Clark said, "No, didn't you?"

Charles said, "No, I didn't shoot." They both looked at me, then Charles asked, "Did you shoot?" I told them I had shot with the .22 but couldn't believe I had killed that crow. We went over and picked up the dead crow. Not only had I killed it, but I had hit it directly underneath its beak and the bullet had exited through the top of its head! It was sheer luck. I just wasn't that good of a marksman. As a matter of fact, it really wasn't the crow I was aiming for; I never told Charles and Clark that!

We continued to hunt almost every day after school, being very careful to avoid trespassing on Jim's land. All the farm animals were now gone except for the chickens, and there wasn't a lot of evening chores to do. Dad seemed concerned about how he could have a big garden next spring without a horse. One weekend, when James came home to visit, he told Dad he should consider buying one of these new garden tractors. James said he knew someone who had a used garden tractor for sale and he could bring it up for Dad to try out. It sounded great. During the winter, it wouldn't have to be fed or watered.

On his next trip home, James brought the garden tractor up to the farm on a small trailer. It had handles to guide and control it which looked very similar to a turning plow's handles. If you pressed down on the left handle the tractor would go to the left, and if you pressed down on the right handle the tractor would turn to the right. The operator would walk between the two handles directly behind the tractor. James, Dad, and I took the garden tractor out in the garden area to try it out. James started the gasoline engine. The turning plow was attached to the tractor. Then James engaged the clutch. The little tractor was far too wimpy to pull the turning plow through the heavy clay garden soil. It began to bounce up and down and the tires were spinning but the tractor wasn't moving forward. James moved the handles up and down in an effort to get the tractor to zigzag from side to side, hopeful that it would help the tractor to begin moving forward. It got away from James and began taking off across the garden. James and I caught up to it, and James was able to disengage the clutch and kill the engine. Dad stood watching all this commotion. He said, "A man could get killed by that blooming thing. I wouldn't give a dime for that contraption. Maybe I'll look for a small mule just for my garden."

I overheard Mother and Dad talking one day about Aunt Kate and Uncle Oscar considering asking the government to bring Dugan's body back from overseas. In a way it seemed like it would be a good thing, but in another way, I thought about all that grief and why go through it again? Maybe it would be a good thing to have Dugan home, even if it was for his burial, at least he would be home and not in some foreign land. After much discussion, Kate and Oscar chose to have Dugan's remains returned home.

There would be no funeral service at a church or funeral home, just a military funeral at the grave site. I thought about not going to the funeral, but I thought that would be disrespectful. I decided to go, but I stood some distance away from the grave site. The casket was brought from the hearse by seven soldiers in their dress uniforms. Three on each side and one directly behind the casket. The steel grey casket was covered by a large American flag draped over it. The soldiers gently placed the casket on the mechanism used to lower it into the ground. The drill sergeant then ordered the soldiers into formation to fire their guns. The soldiers fired, then reloaded, and fired a second and third time.

Aunt Kate was crying again, just as much, if not more, than the first time I had watched as she had gotten the telegram informing her of Dugan's death. Nine years had not diminished the agony and grief of this mother who had lost her child. It was a warm morning but again I felt cold and clammy. In the background a bugler began to softly play "Taps." (A call for the dead to rest in peace.) Everyone was standing rigidly with heads bowed. The American flag was then removed from the casket, carefully folded by the soldiers, and then presented to Aunt Kate. A minister offered up a prayer.

Katherine and Bob Meyers gently took their grieving mother away to a waiting car. It was over. Dugan now had a calm and peaceful place to rest. It was good to have him home. Welcome home, Dugan. I've visited that cemetery many times since that day. I always go by Dugan's grave each visit. I'll never forget the ultimate sacrifice this brave young soldier made for our freedom. I just need to say thank you every opportunity I get.

Charles had gotten a job in one of the grocery stores in the small town. He now worked every afternoon when he got out of school. He also worked every Saturday. Our time for hanging out was more limited now. Sometimes I would go over and wait for the store to close, then Charles and I would go to the early movie at the Pastime Theater. Other times, a group of teenage boys could always be found hanging out at the small town drinking fountain across from the main street. The drinking fountain had a shelter over it, and there were sitting benches underneath a protective cover. Some boys who now had access to cars would park along the parking spaces by the drinking fountain. It was customary for the boys to just park and sit in their cars along the front street and listen to a popular radio station which broadcast from Cincinnati, Ohio.

Occasionally, a car load of girls would cruise down the main street, and two or three cars full of boys would fall in behind the girls. The boys would show off by screeching their tires, revving their engines, or charging up very fast behind the girls and then braking very quickly. (Just normal teenagers doing crazy things.) I envied the city boys who had their dad's fancy cars. The girls were drawn to those nice cars like buzzards to road kill! I had to be content with sitting on a bench underneath the drinking fountain canopy. I assessed the advantage of having a nice car and money in your pocket when it came to attracting a girl. I thought, if I study really hard and get good grades, maybe one day I can get a good job and a nice car. Then I'll have to fight the girls off with a stick!

Shortly after school was out in May 1951, Charles came over to hang out. He was unusually quiet and seemed troubled by something. I asked him, "What's up?"

Charles blurted out, "We're moving to Detroit." I was stunned by this news. There had been no talk about moving. Charles stated his older brothers were doing well in Detroit, and they could get him a good-paying job there. His brother, Bob, had enough room in his house for their mother, Mattie, Clarence, Charles, and Peggy to come and live with him and his wife and baby. They would be moving in another week. Another friend lost. Would I ever see Charles again? Charles's move to Detroit was interrupted by his being drafted into the army.

Very shortly after arriving in Detroit, Charles was drafted and sent to France for two years. He had a great time in the army and thoroughly enjoyed Paris. His primary duty in the army was driving a supply truck. In the fall of 1952, I entered the tentth grade. For one of my electives, I chose vocational agriculture. This was a double-hour subject, and the vocational agriculture class was located in a separate building directly behind the high school. I knew when I selected this class that I had no intentions of ever becoming a farmer when I finished school. Most of the older boys, however, said it was a very easy subject and you got to go on many field trips.

Mr. White was the voc. ag. teacher. It just so happened that in 1952, Mr. White was also appointed as interim superintendent of schools. This new duty consumed most of his time.

Each day he would rush out to the voc. ag. building and tell us to read a chapter in a text book and answer the questions at the end of the chapter or else he would have one of the boys operate a slide projector and show slide films for about an hour. Generally, Mr. White wouldn't stay at the voc. ag. building but very briefly, he had too many duties in the main office as acting superintendent. This class was more than easy; it was a piece-of-cake easy!

One day, Mr. White stayed for the entire period. He sat us all down at the beginning of the class and asked the question, "What does it mean to castrate a pig?" Of course, the rural boys knew what it meant but had never ever heard it brought up in a discussion before. One boy, trying to be knowledgeable stated, "It means to cut them." This term was usually used by the farmers instead of the technical term *castrate*.

Mr. White then asked, "What do you mean by 'to cut them'?"

Another boy chimed in with, "It means to neuter them."

Again Mr. White asked, "What does it mean to neuter them?"

Silence.

Mr. White was now ready with the proper explanation. "It means to surgically remove the testicles from the animal." He then asked if anyone knew why this was done. The questions had now advanced beyond any tenth grade boy's knowledge. Nobody had ever gone this far into the details of castrating an animal. Mr. White then pulled out his slide projector and began a slide presentation, in living color, on the proper procedure for castrating a pig. Every boy sat spellbound, knees clamped firmly together, and hands over their crouch!

After the fifteen-minute presentation, Mr. White asked if there were any questions. One boy, feeling a great deal of empathy for the pig, asked, "Doesn't that hurt?"

Mr. White smiled and said, "It doesn't hurt at all. I've never felt any pain."

He then said, "Oh, you're asking if it hurt the pig? Of course it hurts the pig, didn't you hear it squealing?"

Over the next three or four weeks, we went on many field trips out to various farms to castrate pigs. (Farmers liked to have the boys do it because it was done free as part of their class instruction.) Why was it necessary? Mr. White explained that the male hormones produced by the testicles in male pigs and bulls made the meat very strong flavored and tough, therefore, unfit for good quality meat. He also explained that uncastrated male animals could become very aggressive and dangerous if uncastrated. This was just another experience which convinced me that I would never, never, never ever be a farmer.

Of course, being on the farm, the rural children were constantly exposed to mating by all sorts of fowl and animals; usually at the most inopportune time. Rest assured, if a group of adults were sitting on the front porch visiting with each other, this would be the precise time the old Rhode Island Red Rooster would chase down a hen right out in the front yard. All the adults would look away, pretending not to be aware at all as to what was happening while at the same time sneaking a peek at the copulation taking place. Talking about sex or sexuality was strictly taboo. Most sex education was learned from the older boys; never at home or even in the schools.

In May 1952, I turned sixteen years old. I now was eligible to get a driver's license. Dad's old truck could not be used to take my driving test due to so many mechanical problems being wrong with it. I did learn to drive using that old truck. Dad would allow me to drive it up and down our lane but never on the main road. Finally, I convinced him to let me drive on the main road while he was in the truck with me.

He wasn't a very comfortable passenger when I drove on the main road. When I went to take my driver's license road test, I borrowed Mr. White's new pickup truck. It was the first time I had ever driven anything but Dad's old truck. It handled so well compared to Dad's old truck that I passed my road test without a hitch. At age sixteen, I could now legally work if I could find a job. A small grocery store and gas station was just south of the small town on the road going up to the ridge. As I walked back and forth from the small town, sometimes I would stop in this store and buy a cold drink or, as everyone called it, a coke. People would come in the store and the clerk would ask, "What would you like?"

The customer would say, "I'll have a coke."

The clerk would then ask, "What flavor coke would you like?"

The customer would then say, "I'll have an orange coke."

The small store and gas station was owned by a single middle-aged man named Dickie Wilkerson, who lived in Bynum Camp. His sister, Sara, also worked in the store. They had built up a very good business in that small store. One day, as I stopped in the store, I asked Dickie if he needed any help at the store. He asked if I had a driver's license. I assured him that I was a licensed driver, and he said he could use some help on Saturdays pumping gas and delivering groceries. I was very happy to now have a job and earn some money. I hurried home and told Mother about my job. I no longer needed to ask Mother's permission to do things. I pretty much just informed her of what I was doing or planned to do. I would say, "I'm going to town," or "I'll be back about dark." She no longer questioned where I was going or what I was going to do. It was up to me to make my own choices, but I still always felt an unspoken rule which dictated what I could and couldn't do. "Don't embarrass our families' reputation. Keep out of trouble and be respectful of others and their property."

I began working at the Wilkerson's store on Saturdays. It was always very busy. I pumped gas, cleaned windshields, and checked under the hood. Gasoline was selling for fifteen cents per gallon. About 10:00 a.m., there would be a truck load of groceries needing to be delivered. I would load them in Dickie's truck, then outline a route I should go to prevent overlapping as much as possible. Dickie and Sara were both very nice. Often as I would get ready to leave with the load of groceries, Dickie would grab an RC Cola from the cooler and hand it to me. Anytime I was in the store and Dickie decided he wanted a snack, he would always toss me something as well. When I would return from delivering the groceries about 1:00 p.m., Dickie would say, "come on, Let's go to lunch."

We would go over to his home in Bynum Camp where his mother, Ma Wilkerson, would have a delicious meal prepared. Ma Wilkerson always had a steady stream of Bynum Camp children coming to her house for a sandwich or snack. She would give them all food from Dickie's store. I don't remember what my pay was for working at the store. It didn't matter anyway. I gave Mother all the money. I figured if I kept it myself it would be gone very quickly. Mother was very good at managing the money.

I worked about a year for the Wilkersons. Then something strange happened; Dickie got married! He'd never talked about a girlfriend or dating, and I thought he was a confirmed bachelor. The young woman he married was obviously pregnant. She began to work at the store, and Sara no longer worked there. Dickie's wife was obviously very inexperienced at working in a grocery store and was not friendly and polite to the customers. Due to her inexperience, when customers would come into the store, she would not warmly greet them and many times just ignore them. Very soon all the customers stopped coming to the store. Business was now very slow and Dickie informed me that he no longer needed me to work on Saturdays. Within a year after Dickie married, the store closed.

Once, on one of my grocery delivery routes while working for the Wilkersons, I went to a rural farm where a man was raising game chickens. These were roosters bred for fighting. I don't know why but I was intrigued with these birds. I asked the farmer if he would sell me some of these eggs from the game chickens. He sold me a dozen of these eggs. Just like with the duck eggs, I put these game chicken eggs under a brooding hen and hatched them. These game cocks had long, spindly legs and rather small bodies. Within six weeks after hatching, these roosters were already fighting each other.

They were very aggressive toward any other roosters. I had to build separate pens for each rooster to keep them separated from each other. Our old Rhode Island Red rooster was now a paranoid coward. Although about three times bigger than the game cocks, he was totally bullied by them. He quit crowing because every time he would crow, one of the game cocks would seek him out and attack him. He spent most of the daylight hours hiding under the house. One of the game cocks eventually became the dominant rooster, and now all the other roosters refused to fight him. He was the king of the hill, and now all the other roosters could be freed from the pens since they all stayed clear of this dominant rooster.

Occasionally, one of the other roosters would get brave or foolish enough to challenge this dominant rooster, and there would be a bloody fight, which Dad didn't like. He was really unhappy about my hobby of raising these fighting chickens. He didn't, however, order me to get rid of them. I was now old enough to decide what I should or shouldn't do. Lois was now dating Bobby, and Bobby could be counted upon to come to the farm two or three weekends a month from Henderson, Tennessee. Bobby was studying to become a minister. Once when he came to see Lois, she was committed to do something that Saturday morning, so Bobby was stuck hanging out with me. Bobby saw the dominant game cock strutting around the barn yard and began asking questions about these chickens. I told Bobby this dominant rooster had never been defeated in a fight. Lois had told Bobby that Monroe Stovall's big Dominecker rooster had become very aggressive toward the children when they walked by Monroe's old house. Lois was very fearful of this old rooster. Bobby asked if I thought this game cock could teach Monroe's Dominecker a lesson and stop him from chasing all the girls. I was absolutely certain my game cock could teach that old Dominecker a thing or two about his attacking the girls.

I put the game cock under my arm, and Bobby and I walked over to Monroe's old house. We heard the Dominecker crow down in the woods in front of Monroe's house. My game cock heard it as well. The feathers on his neck flared out, and he struggled to get free of my grasp. When the Dominecker crowed again, I dropped the game cock to the ground. He bounded away in the direction where the Dominecker had crowed. Soon we heard loud squawking. Then much more squawking! Something interesting was going on down in the woods. Then we spotted that ole Dominecker running as fast as he could toward Monroe's house. The game cock was right behind him, and when he would catch up, he would leap on the ole Dominecker's back, and those grey speckled feathers were flying from the Dominecker's back and he was loudly squawking. Fearful that Monroe might be home and see what was going on, I quickly ran over and caught my game cock. The ole Dominecker continued running for cover under the house.

Bobby laughed all the way back home. We didn't tell anyone else about this. Bobby thought it might not be proper conduct for a future preacher. Bobby still laughed about this every time he came to see Lois and saw that dominant game cock strutting around the barn yard. Dad was still very unhappy with all the rooster fights going on around the barn. I think he was secretly thinking of how he could get rid of these roosters. One day, Mother asked Dad to kill a chicken for our evening meal. Dad took the .22 rifle out to the barn yard to kill a chicken. He came back into the house with my prized dominant rooster he had shot. He stated, "I think I might have shot the wrong rooster." There was nothing I could do about it now, the rooster was dead. It didn't taste very good either!

The Korean War was now raging. Everyone was fearful it might escalate into World War III. Was nuclear war right around the corner? Even though Fred was just finishing his apprenticeship at the Redstone Arsenal, he was drafted into the army. He was sent to Germany and served as a machinist on a large portable machine shop in West Berlin. Fortunately, he wasn't sent to Korea to fight in the bitter cold and snow. Charles was now in the army as well. Frankie was the only friend still on the ridge.

Frankie's mother still kept tight control over Frankie's whereabouts. Now we didn't hang out too much. Now with the Wilkerson store closed, I had much idle time on my hands. I decided to check with some other stores, hopeful of getting another job. After being turned down at several stores, finally Burgess Grocery Store hired me to work on Saturdays. I was basically doing the same thing I had done at the Wilkerson store. Burgess grocery was also a very busy store on Saturdays. Their son, Glen, and I would deliver all the groceries. Glen was a year older than me. By 10:00 a.m., there would be a truck load of groceries and animal feed ready to be delivered. We usually would not get back before about 1:00 p.m.

Once back, there would be another truck load of orders ready to be delivered. Usually we would not get back from our afternoon delivery until about 6:00 p.m. Many people, even those in the small town, would call in their orders instead of coming to the store and getting the groceries themselves. My work hours on Saturday were from 8:00 a.m. until 9:00 p.m. and I earned five dollars. I was very glad to have that job. It was very heavy work. Most of the rural folks would order two or three one-hundred-pound bags of cow feed or pig feed. Oftentimes when we would get to their farms, they would tell us to put the sacks of feed up in the barn. Most times this would be up a very steep pathway about two hundred feet away. By the time we were finished delivering the groceries and all the feed, we would have a heavy cake of cow feed and sweat on our necks and shoulders. Sometimes if it were slow in the store, Glen and I would go in the back of the store where all the one-hundred-pound bags of cow feed were stacked and see who could lift a one-hundred-pound bag of cow feed over our heads the most times. (So full of energy at sixteen and seventeen.)

I still felt obligated to turn my earnings over to Mother. This would help with the family expenses. If there were essential things I really needed, like something for school, I would ask Mother if there was enough money for me to get what I needed. Often she would come up with the money. I never knew where she kept the money. It was hidden somewhere in the house. I don't think Dad even knew where the money was hidden.

Jerry Files was now in college. Since his Dad, Edger, had gotten a lot of money from the strip mining of their land, all the Files boys were fortunate enough to go to college directly after graduating from high school. Jerry was a cadet in the ROTC while attending college. One night after we had all gone to bed, a huge military airplane came flying very low over the mountain. Suddenly the bright landing lights came on, and the airplane's engines began to rev up very loudly. We all ran out of the house. We thought this plane was going to crash. It, however, continued on its way. A few days later, we found out Jerry was on that plane, and he had talked the pilot into strafing the mountain. I imagine he would have been in big trouble if anyone had reported this incident.

In the summer of 1953, Lois went back down to Jacksonville to work in a store while school was out. Bobby was also home from college for the summer and worked at the college doing maintenance work. Our senior high school year was coming up in the fall, and Lois and I both knew we would need extra money for things like a class ring, class pic-

LOUIS ELLIOTT

tures, and a class trip to Florida. I went to Birmingham and
stayed with James, hoping I could find a summer job. I was
hired at a grocery store called Bruno's Market. Mr. Bruno's
wife sat in an elevated office at one end of the store. From
there she could observe everything going on in the store.
From this elevated position, she was constantly yelling at all
the employees. "Dust the shelves, sweep the floor, stock the
shelves, answer the phone, etc., etc."

Within my first hour of work, I had grown to hate her.
I was very glad to see James when he picked me up that evening. I told him I would never go back to that place to work.
All the store employees were Negroes, and I began to understand how very mistreated they were. People like Dickie
Wilkerson's wife and Mrs. Bruno needed to learn how to
respect and treat their fellow man. Why did they feel a need
to be so rude and unpleasant? They offended everyone who
worked for them, and just importantly, they were destroying
their own livelihood and didn't realize it. I thought, I'd rather
do without some of my senior functions rather than endure
Mrs. Bruno's abuse.

I was happy to get back home from Birmingham.
I decided to take a walk down No. 11 Hill and do some
thinking. I stopped by a family's house that were planning
on moving very soon. They had a pretty daughter about a
year younger than me. There was no need to take any interest in Virginia Farmer; she would be gone in about another
week. The Farmers had lived there only a short while, maybe
two years, and now they were moving again. I don't know
where they moved. Mr. Farmer asked me if I knew anyone
that might be interested in buying his mule and wagon. By
now almost no one was interested in buying a mule. Tractors
of various sizes and horsepower had almost totally replaced

mules and horses. I told him I didn't know anyone interested in buying his mule.

On the way home, I stopped to watch a group of loggers cutting off a section of timber in a very rugged section of woods. They had a large logging truck loaded with logs down in a steep ravine. The road they had made to drive the truck up out of the ravine was very steep. I watched as the truck started laboring up the steep grade with the heavy load of logs. As it got to the steepest part of the road, there was a loud bang which came from the truck's engine. Smoke and steam began to billow out from under the hood. The engine had blown a head gasket. The truck stalled and wouldn't start up again. The loggers decided the hill was just too steep to use a truck. They asked me if I knew anyone around there with a horse they could hire to skid the logs up out of the ravine. I stated, "Yes, I've got a mule and I'm an experienced log skidder." They then told me if I wanted a job, I could start work tomorrow morning.

I turned around and went back to the Farmer's house. I asked what he was asking for his mule. He told me he would sell the mule and wagon for twenty-five dollars. I told him I would be back in about two hours with the money. I think I had about twenty dollars saved for my senior class expenses. I asked Mother if I could borrow another five dollars so I could buy Farmer's mule. I explained that I had a job offer to skid logs for twenty dollars per day. Mother agreed to give me the money.

I took the money and hurried back down to Mr. Farmers to buy the mule, sight unseen. I gave the money to Mr. Farmer and went around to the barn to claim my mule. When I saw the mule I thought, "That's the ugliest mule I've ever seen!" She had the biggest, longest head I'd ever seen on a mule. Her ears were huge and floppy. She was potbellied and her legs looked scrawny compared to her body. I doubted she would be capable of skidding heavy logs up a steep hillside. I thought I'd made a bad mistake by purchasing this mule. Maybe I could sell the wagon to an antique dealer and get my money back.

I hitched ole Nell to the wagon and drove it home. She was a very gentle mule and obeyed my commands very well. I unhitched Nell from the wagon and put her in Dolly's old stall. I had to raid the chicken house to get some shelled corn for Nell to eat. I hoped she would be strong for the next day's work. Early the next morning, I harnessed ole Nell with her collar and skidding chains. I then rode her back down No. 11 Hill to the work site. I think I heard one of the men snickering at that ugly mule and the young experienced skidder. The men showed me where they wanted the logs to be stacked when they were skidded up from the steep hill. I just prayed ole Nell would be able to pull the logs.

I took her down into the ravine and selected a medium-sized log to hook the skidding tongs into. Using the reins, I had to walk very near the log and close behind the mule. Holding the reins firmly, I told ole Nell to, "Git up." She began pulling and responded to my reins as I guided her up the steep slope. There was no quitting in ole Nell. Not once all day did I hook her to a log she couldn't pull! She had amazing strength and stamina.

The loggers were very pleased with the work we did that day. That evening, as I rode ole Nell back home, I kept patting her on the neck. I didn't care if she was ugly; she was a mighty fine mule! That night I gave her an extra portion of shelled corn. For the next several days, Nell and I worked, skidding those logs up the steep slope. I thought I had to guide and control ole Nell as we skidded the logs. Sometimes I had to run to keep up with the mule. It seemed, the bigger the log, the faster ole Nell went. One day as I was walking beside a log and holding the reins, I tripped over a tree root and fell. I had to quickly roll away to keep the log from hitting me as I lay on the ground. I let go of the reins and ole Nell kept going. To my surprise she pulled the log all the way up the slope and stopped at the place we were stacking the logs. I wondered if she would do that again.

When we went back down into the ravine for another log, I hitched her into another log and told Nell to "Git up." I then let go of the reins and watched as Nell pulled the log all the way up to the stack of logs and stopped again. This was great; it made it so much easier for me. A day later, however, I discovered the downside of this new skidding method. I attached a short lead line about two feet long on Nell's bridle. This was sufficient to lead her back down into the ravine and short enough that it wouldn't get caught on a bush or tree limb.

The skidding tongs are similar to ice tongs except much stronger. They are designed in an X-shape with a strong chain across the top of the X and the other ends were bent inward at a ninety degree angle and sharpened. As the horse or mule tightens the chain as it begins to pull, the sharpened points dig into the log and usually hold tight as long as the mule is pulling. Occasionally, however, if the log hits a buried tree root or rock, the tongs can be ripped out of the log, thus separating the mule from the log it's pulling. Since I was no longer using the long reins, I had no control of ole Nell when the tongs would rip out of a log. Nell would sense when this would happen, and instead of stopping, she would keep going all the way back to her stall in the barn! I couldn't catch her. She would run just fast enough so that I couldn't catch her. After this happened on three consecutive days. I was very angry and frustrated with that mule. I smacked her in the nose with my fist. It didn't help; the next day she did it again. I decided I'd better put the long reins back on her (problem solved).

I worked about three weeks with the loggers before their timber cutting in this section was completed. I had earned three hundred dollars. The loggers informed me that they would be moving to a new section about fifteen miles away. They asked if I would be interested in a job at the new location. I told them I wouldn't be able to work that far away. The loggers then asked I would be interested in selling ole Nell. I stated, "If you will take good care of her and don't overwork her or abuse her, I'll sell her to you for thirty-five dollars."

The logger said, "Sold." I probably should have asked for more money! Now I had a wagon and no mule to pull it!

Dad's old truck was falling apart. It was difficult to start and heavy black smoke was coming from the exhaust pipe. It wasn't going to run much longer. One day, as we went to the county seat to do some shopping, I noticed a fine looking 1946 Chevrolet on a used car lot. The price was six hundred dollars. I told Mother and Dad that I would give them the three hundred dollars I had earned skidding those logs to put toward the purchase of that car. Fred was now in the army and stationed in Germany. Each month he would send most of his army pay back home for Mother to put it in the bank for him. Mother said she would write a letter to Fred and see if he would loan us the rest of the money needed to get that car. Fred replied to the letter and said it would be okay to borrow the money from his saving account. We finally had a decent looking car and now I might be able to pick up some chicks!

Lois had returned to Jacksonville to work during the summer months. She lived with Vera and Garland and of course spent much time with Bobby as he returned to his summer maintenance job at Jacksonville State Teacher's College. Since I had now spent all my earnings on the car, I was now broke. The extra money needed for our senior year's expenses was gone. It looked as if I wouldn't be able to afford the senior class ring or senior trip to Florida. Lois told me she had saved enough money from her job in Jacksonville to pay the senior expenses for both of us! I loved my twin sister!

Our senior year was very busy and time was rapidly moving forward toward graduation. I sometimes regretted being a senior and being finished with school. It was a good place, a fun place, a secure place. Many of the rural boys had already left school. When they reached sixteen years old, they had had enough schooling. They quit to take jobs as loggers, truck drivers, or coal miners. Others joined the military even though there was the possibility they might end up fighting in Korea. If they were good football players, however, the coach managed to keep them in school until after football season was over. One of our football players was even married!

Now that I had a decent car available, I spent some evenings parked along the front street of the small town. Other teenagers would congregate there as well. I must admit that at times this would be boring, but there wasn't much else to do. I couldn't afford the cost of gasoline to do very much cruising.

I was president of the Honor Society in my senior year. Students from the tenth to twelfth grades were chosen for this distinction and honor if they maintained a B or better grade average and were considered model citizens. About midterm, a young tenth grade girl transferred to our school. She was very pretty and very intelligent. She was inducted into the honor society. As president, I was directed to orient

Frances to the various responsibilities and duties of the honor society members. Did I say she was pretty? Pretty, confident, fairly quiet, unpretentious, mature, and pretty! I began seeking her out each day, just in case she had questions about the honor society. Our friendship grew and other students began to notice. It was only a friendship; after all, she was barely sixteen, but I thought, a mature sixteen.

As the school year approached its end, I had been on a few dates with Frances. But it was mostly just sitting on her porch and talking. There were several seniors that were now couples. Some had been dating since tenth grade. I thought no doubt some of these couples would be married soon. There must have been a sudden jolt of reality surging through the school as the school year approached its end. There were many breakups of these couples. It was very emotional times for these stressed out students. Were we prepared for the next phase of our lives? Are we ready to move on? Only three more weeks of school, then what? The seniors would leave on their senior trip to Florida next week. Before leaving on the class trip, I decided I would ask Frances if she would like to go to the movies Friday night. It was fairly late in the evening when I drove up to her house. I asked her if she'd like to go with me to the movies. She stated, "I'm sorry, I already have a date Friday night."

I felt like ole Nell had kicked me in the stomach. I didn't expect that answer. I searched for words but nothing appropriate seemed to come to mind. I simply sputtered, "Okay, maybe I'll see you when I get back from our class trip."

I tried to be very cavalier about this. "Oh well, there's plenty of other girls out there, no big deal." It's something you don't discuss with others. It's so private and hurtful to you, but to everyone else, it's just not important. It happens all the time. How do you get over it and move on? I thought

about the future. What's just around the bend in the road?
I don't know, but I'm so ready to find out! I drove back to
the small town and parked on the main street. It was now
getting dark. There was a car full of teenagers already parked
there. Their radio was blaring from station WCKY from
Cincinnati, Ohio. Don Gibson was wailing out his popular
song, "Oh, Lonesome Me."

> Well, there must be someway
> I can lose these lonesome blues,
> Forget the past and find somebody new.
> I've thought of everything from A to Z.
> Oh, lonesome me.
> I bet she's not like me, she's out and fancy free,
> Flirting with the boys with all her charms.
> A bad mistake I'm making by just hang-
> ing around.
> I know I should have some fun and paint
> the town.
> A love sick fool is blind and just can't see,
> Oh, lonesome me!

I tried to rationalize. "She's only sixteen, just a child
still." She has a right to date anyone she wishes. I have no
control over what she chooses to do. It probably would have
ended sooner or later anyway with school being out for the
summer and all. It was a friendship, nothing serious. It's time
to move on; but where? What does the future have in store
for me? I didn't have a clue. The school had been my rock
and security blanket for twelve years. But now it won't be
there any longer. I'll have to make most decisions alone. How
can I find a job? I've only been out of the state of Alabama
one other time. I've never ventured any further away than the

two-hour trip to Birmingham. Bring on the future; I'm so ready to leave this small town and this ole mountain!

The plan was for the Greyhound bus to leave the high school parking lot at 6:00 p.m. Thursday evening on our senior class trip. The seniors were to sleep on the bus all night and arrive in Jacksonville, Florida, about 9:00 a.m. fresh and rested and ready to hit the beach. There were no expressways, and it would require ten or eleven hours of driving time plus rest stops.

Everyone was very excited as the bus pulled away from the high school parking lot. Songs such as, "Home on the Range," "You Are My Sunshine," and "Hey, Good Looking" were sung over and over. Seats were traded back and forth as seniors shared time together. As the evening changed into night, the lights inside the bus were turned off. The bus began to get quieter and the kids began to settle down for the night. I fluffed my pillow and stuffed it between the seat and the bus window. The bus wasn't crowded, and so I had the double seat to myself. I stretched out across the two seats and dozed off.

It was now dark. Some low conversations could still be heard from various areas on the bus. I sensed someone taking the aisle seat next to me. Then a girl lay across my chest and snuggled her head underneath my chin. It felt good! Not in any making out way but very much like a small child would snuggle in the arms of its mother or father. The bus was chilly and I felt the girl's arms. They were cool and I placed my arms across hers to help keep her comfortable. She gently snuggled her head under my chin, expressing her appreciation for my thoughtfulness. Soon I could tell by her slow, steady breathing that she had fallen asleep. I fell asleep as well.

I awoke about three hours later and the girl was gone. Who was that girl? I had my suspicions but wasn't certain.

As daylight appeared, I searched for clues in the girls' faces. None seemed to show signs which would have betrayed the mystery girl. I thought about how very close we had all become during our twelve years together.

Soon this would all be over. We would no longer have each other to lean upon. There would surely be empty places in our hearts for some of our high school buddies. We arrived in Jacksonville and had a great three or four days on the beach. One night, a patrol car chased us off the beach at 1:00 a.m. because we were doing the bunny hop. Some older retirees in their beach condos were cussing us. Some suffered painful sunburns and others drove the resort manager crazy by partying all night.

We returned home very tired and exhausted. We had only a short time to recover before graduation. It was great fun, but now the reality of graduation day was upon us. All the graduates were emotional wrecks. Many of us had been together since first grade. All were crying and hugging and trying to be brave. This is the last time ever that we will be together as a class. It was if that school building sitting so majestically upon the hill top overlooking the small town was now rejecting us. "You're no longer welcome here, go away."

I didn't sleep well that night after graduation; too much on my mind. The next morning, I took a walk up the lane and sat down on the large flat rock (my thinking place). I looked up and saw a single crow flying in a straight line high above the mountain. There were no other crows in the pine trees calling and beckoning him to fly down and join them. No ripe juicy ears of fat corn tempting him in the fields. No corn at all, just fields overgrown with thistle weeds, prairie grass, and saw briers. Time to keep flying; perhaps things will be better as I fly further and further away from this ole mountain. I watched in silence as the crow became just a small black speck against the clear blue morning sky. Then he was gone.

The next Saturday, as usual, I went to work at Burgess's grocery store. Their son, Glenn, who was a year older than me decided he would go to summer school at college. He would not be back to work at the grocery store that summer. George Burgess asked if I would be interested in working full time at the grocery store. Having nothing else planned for my immediate future, I gladly accepted the job offer. I worked from 8:00 a.m. until 5:30 p.m., Monday through Friday and from 8:00 a.m. until 9:00 p.m. on Saturdays. My pay was twenty-five dollars per week. The Burgess grocery store had hired one of the town locals, Joe McDonald, as their butcher just before I started working full time. Joe was a happy-go-lucky man who laughed and joked with everyone who came into the store. He was a perfect store clerk who enjoyed his job very much. Joe harbored no prejudice against the Negroes. He treated them exactly the same way as he did the white folks. Within three months, almost all the Negroes from the small town did their shopping at Burgess's grocery store. The business grew tremendously with Joe working there. Dickie Wilkerson's wife and Mrs. Bruno could have learned a great deal about how to manage a business from Joe. Unfortunately Joe was trapped in a camping trailer fire while on a fishing trip and died a tragic death.

Lois went back down to Jacksonville just after graduation. She enrolled in college there, but I suspected it was more about being where Bobby was rather than being about college. One weekend, Bobby brought Lois back home for a weekend visit. Bobby always stayed at a church member's home in the small town when he visited the farm. He would never stay at the farm before they were married. On this particular visit, Lois and Bobby brought one of Bobby's nieces with them. They were trying to play cupid. This girl was attractive and, as they say, had a great personality. They thought they would strike up a romance between me and his niece. Too bad the timing was all wrong. I tried to show some interest in that girl, and we sat on the front porch swing and held hands. My mind still was swirling around the way things had ended between Frances and me. Even though it didn't go very well that weekend, the niece expressed to Lois that she was still interested in seeing me again. It just never worked out.

I decided about a week after Lois and Bobby and the niece visited that I might just cruise by Frances's house and just say hi. I drove up to the house, but it was empty. The family had moved. I wondered about the date she said she had the night she couldn't go to the movies. Was it real or was this her way of handling all that was on her mind? At sixteen, young girls don't always think logically. They still have a lot of maturing to do. What they think is best may not always be the best, but they still have a right to make their own decisions. It was her life and I had to respect her decision. Close this chapter, it's time to move on. I thought of the numerous losses I'd experienced in my life. The loss of good friends, relatives, grandmothers and grandfathers, and even the animals on the farm. Every segment of my life I had experienced losses. Life presents many unexpected and grievous losses. Beyond the next bend in the road, however, may be marvelous and exciting experiences and opportunities. If we seize these new opportunities, we will be rewarded for our ability to hang in there and taste the sweet victories of success.

That summer was lonely on the farm. Six of the seven children were now gone. I missed them all but especially Lois. Why were all my brothers and sisters so far away?

The farm itself had changed. Kudzu began creeping up the hills and pasture. Soon it would overtake the pig pen. If left unchecked, the kudzu would slowly and steadily overtake the trees, the fields, and even the outbuildings. Kudzu is a rapidly growing vine which was introduced in this area as a way to control soil erosion on the hill sides and ravines. Once established, it has to be battled continuously to prevent it from overtaking everything in its path. What was thought to be a good idea had now turned into a nightmare. Kudzu was choking and killing the trees. It crept over idle fields. Now it was threating to overtake the barn and garden area. Kudzu had now totally overtaken Monroe's old house. It covered the outbuildings still standing at the old McDonald's homestead. In early spring, the children looked forward to picking the wild pansies with their velvety smooth blossoms of yellow, purple, and brown which formed a cascade of color on the hill behind Ma Elliott's homestead. Wild azaleas and sweet Williams welcomed spring as they flourished amid the crevices and rocks along No. 11 Hill. Now all were gone. Only heavy, thick, choking kudzu covers the hills.

As fall approached, Lois and Bobby announced they planned to be married in December. I attended their wedding after a morning worship service at the Sixth Avenue Church of Christ in Jasper on December 16, 1954. Old time gospel preacher Gus Nichols officiated at their wedding. The ceremony was simple and only about fifteen minutes long. Bobby was just finishing his college education and had accepted a minister's position with the Mumford Church of Christ.

Lois would no longer be living at home. Now the only child left at home from the seven was me. I felt as if I were an unfinished picture on an artist's canvas. There were so many unfinished strokes of the artist's brush. Key parts were unfinished. I needed to complete the painting, but how and where? Mother sensed my restlessness. Like a young eaglet ready to leave the nest, Mother sensed that it was almost time for me to fly away. Time to leave the nest and soar away beyond this ole mountain to adventures yet unexplored.

It was two days past Christmas 1954. I sat on the front porch gazing to the east watching the sun rise up over the hills and valleys. I wondered how many times in my life I had gazed across these hills and valleys in the early morning. Nonetheless, each time it was a refreshing and beautiful scene. I was distracted by a car coming up the road. Billows of dry dust rose up into the air from beneath the car. It was traveling unusually fast. Ridge folks don't normally drive this fast unless there's an emergency. The car abruptly slowed and turned into our lane. As it approached our house, I noticed it was a beautiful brand-new Chevrolet. The car stopped in front of our house and the door popped open. Charles Thornbro stepped from the car and smiled and waved to me while I was still sitting on the porch. I couldn't believe it! I didn't think when he left in 1951 that I would ever see him again. There he was, smiling and waving just like the three years were only three days.

I ran out to greet Charles. He grabbed my hand and tried to twist it behind my back. I stomped on his big toe! We both began to laugh. Mother and Dad came out of the house to greet Charles. He was excited to tell about his army adventures in France. He had very recently been discharged from the army, and once back in Detroit, he had gotten a good-paying job. We visited for a while and then Charles asked if I would like to go with him down to Bynum Camp to see if he could find some old friends.

I hopped into the shiny new car. It had less than one thousand miles on it. We drove down to Bynum Camp and found Clark. The three of us then went to town and went into the restaurant and ordered a barbeque sandwich. Charles paid the bill. He began telling us about Detroit and all the good jobs there. He said if I would go back with him, he could get me a good-paying job. There was plenty of work in Detroit building all these new cars. I'd never thought about going to Detroit. I was intrigued with the idea. It seemed very exciting, and I told Charles I would think about going back with him. I told Charles I was completely broke and didn't have any money to pay my expense for such a trip. Charles pulled a big wad of money from his pocket and said, "How much do you need? I'll loan you some money and you can stay with us in Detroit."

I asked Charles how long he planned to be in Alabama. He stated he needed to be back in Detroit by January 1. He stated he planned to leave the following Sunday and drive straight through to Detroit. I told Charles I would think about it, and he could come by after church on Sunday, and I would be ready if I decided to go back with him.

When Charles dropped me back off at home, I told Mother and Dad I was thinking about going back to Detroit with Charles. I told them how Charles had assured me I wouldn't have any trouble finding a good-paying job in Detroit. I'd never seen that look on Mother's face before. It appeared to be sad and at the same time happy for the prospects of me getting a job. Tears were in her eyes. Dad said, "Well, if it doesn't work out, you can always come back home." I was very apprehensive, but thought that this is my opportunity! Maybe I should go.

Charles stopped back by again later that day. I told him I'd made up my mind to go back with him. He told me he would be back by about 2:00 p.m. on Sunday to pick me up. I found an old suitcase, which had not been used in years. I gathered up my clothes and my high school diploma. I felt good about my decision to go back with Charles.

Charles arrived promptly at 2:00 p.m. that Sunday. I was packed and ready to go. I hugged Mother and shook Dad's hand. You could sense the emotions Mother was feeling. "My last child is leaving home. He's going far, far away." My heart was heavy as well. I struggled to hold back tears. I quickly tossed the old ragged suitcase into the trunk of Charles car and opened the passenger's door. Mother and Dad watched us intently, standing motionless.

As I got into the car, Mother, through tears and a quivering voice, softly said, "You be sure and write often and let me know how you're doing." Charles backed his new Chevy out into the lane toward the main road. We slowly drove past the old barn. My twenty-five-dollar wagon was still parked underneath the barn overhang. I noticed ole Dolly's collar still hanging on the barn wall. A pair of robins had built a nest in the collar that spring. Now all the robins were gone and the nest was falling apart. Charles turned onto the main road and headed toward the small town. I strained my eyes to take in a final glimpse of all the familiar sights.

Charles began to pick up speed as we headed east away from the small town. I looked in the side rearview mirror. The buildings along the main street were rapidly losing their distinction. Only smears of black and white and grey colors blended together into vague forms. Soon they would be completely gone from sight. Only the outlines of the mountain tops would remain visible until they blended into the bright blue December sky. I stopped looking into the rearview mirror. The road ahead appeared straight and smooth. Charles broke the silence, "By this time tomorrow you will be far, far away from home." I thought, "No, I won't. There will always be a part of that ole mountain in my heart."

Sequel: High School Age

The '50s ushered in one of the most amazing decades of American history. Perhaps due to my just entering my teenage years and becoming more aware of changes taking place all around me, or perhaps due to the expanding volumes of information constantly being provided by the new technology of television, I began to become more and more aware of a very rapidly changing American society. Rural America had begun a magnificent transformation from rural to urban and suburban living. Alabama families living on farms changed from approximately 220,000 in 1950 to only 47,000 by the year 2000. The invention and rapid growth of the television industry enlightened and expanded the horizons for folks still living on the small rural farms and small towns. Massive migrations from rural to urban areas where good-paying job opportunities abounded was due in large part to the information disseminated through television. Shiny new automobiles were appearing in the attached garages on all the subdivision homes being mass produced in areas around all major cities. Rows of mass produced custom homes were introduced in areas like Detroit and Chicago. These homes were being sold as rapidly as they could be built. Most young returning war veterans were getting married and having children. These returning young men took advantage of the low interest, thirty-year, GI mortgages extended to them by the federal government to purchase their dream homes. In 1946, 3.4 million babies were born in America, setting a record for the most births in a single year!

The United States became the world's most powerful military power. However, it was being militarily challenged by the unification of communist nations led by Russia and China. Americans became paranoid with the possibility of the infusion of communist spies and turncoat American scientists suspected of espionage and delivering military secrets to the Communist nations. Senator Joseph McCarthy of Tennessee conducted a series of hearings which were labeled as un-American activities. Sweeping accusations of many prominent American citizens were vigorously debated on the floor of the Senate and were televised daily across the nation. A mistrust and suspicion of fellow citizens led to much distrust between those in Hollywood and the federal government.

The civil rights movement began in the 1950s. Many segregation laws common in southern states were being struck down as unconstitutional by Supreme Court rulings. The Supreme Court declared that laws implementing separate but equal education opportunities in southern states were illegal. Rosa Parks made her famous bus stand and refused to yield her seat to a white man on a public bus in Montgomery, Alabama, in December 1955.

The Cold War heated up significantly during the '50s. The war commonly dubbed the Korean Conflict began in 1950. After three years of horrific fighting and blood shed, a shaky truce was declared in 1953. Thirty-three thousand seven hundred forty two American soldiers lost their lives in this conflict. It is estimated that over one million communist Chinese and North Korean soldiers were killed during this war.

The space age race began in earnest when Russia successfully orbited the first man made satellite in December 1957. This feat caused the United States to initiate a furious catch-up program in space age technology. Huge sums of money were allocated to a program designed to beat the Russians to the moon. Initially, spectacular failures caused much embarrassment for our nation. We did, however, eventually achieve our objective and were the first and only country ever to land a man on the moon.

The Cuban Revolution began in 1954 and ended in 1962 with the overthrow of the Cuban Dictatorship. Fidel Castro established the first Communist government in the Western Hemisphere, less than one hundred miles from our territorial boundary. This added even more tension and volatility to an already simmering conflict between freedom and communism.

The 1950s were dubbed as the Golden Age of Television. On September 4, 1951, President Harry S. Truman made the first transcontinental speech carried live on television from coast to coast. In that same year, the enormously popular comedy series *I Love Lucy* began its weekly broadcast on national television. Some of the older crooners like Frank Sinatra, Bing Crosby, and Tony Bennett remained popular and had their own hit television series. Patti Page, Judy Garland, and Doris Day were among the most popular female vocalist. By 1954, color television made its appearance. The first nationally televised event in living color was the tournament of roses parade in November 1954.

Then in the late '50s, a whole new style of music erupted on television. Chuck Berry, Fats Domino, James Brown, and of course, the one and only Elvis Pressley, ushered in a new era of music to be known as rock and roll.

Television affected all aspects of American life. Dress styles, hair styles, what we ate, what music we listened to, political viewpoints, world news impacts, and changing lifestyles. Hollywood-produced movies were becoming less popular. Folks preferred staying home and watching television in their own living rooms. Frozen TV dinners were invented! These frozen meals became enormously popular as they eliminated the need to prepare meals thus allocating more viewing time for evening television. These frozen meals could be popped into the oven for about thirty minutes, without disrupting valuable television viewing time. Then, utilizing a TV tray, the hot meal could be enjoyed while watching your favorite evening television show. (Never mind the fact that most TV dinners were about as appetizing as last Sunday's leftovers!) Classic Hollywood movies such as *Gentlemen Prefer Blondes*, featuring Marilyn Monroe, *Father of the Bride*, starring Elizabeth Taylor, and *African Queen*, staring Humphrey Bogart, were box office disappointments as people stayed away in droves, being enamored with their televisions.

Jackie Robinson became the first Negro athlete to break the color barrier by joining the Dodger's baseball team in 1954. Willie Mays joined the Giants that same year.

Teenage girls began wearing poodle skirts, pedal pushers, bobby sox, and rolled up jeans. Teenage boys abandoned the GI brush cuts and began allowing their hair to grow long and then slicked back into a duck tail at the back of the head.

Our modern network of freeways and expressways was begun in the 1950s. President Eisenhower is credited with the development of our network of expressways, selling congress on the fact that this would be a vital defense system in case of a communist attempt to launch a land invasion on our borders.

Commercial airlines were now utilizing jet engines for commercial flights. Huge, slick new jet airplanes were transporting three hundred passengers at a time across the country in record breaking time. Air travel became hugely popular and was advertised on television as the only way to travel.

In 1955, Doctor Jonas Salk developed the first successful vaccine effective in preventing polio. Within one year, over seven million school-aged children were vaccinated, sparing, no doubt, thousands of deaths and deformities among our nation's children.

While the country as a whole was enjoying unparalleled prosperity and changing lifestyles, some areas such as the small town and ridge people hardly felt any positive impact on their lives. Most of these changes alluded them. Why had prosperity bypassed this region? First of all, exploitation of this area had run rampant ever since the end of the Civil War. The region was exploited for its natural resources. When the iron ore, coal, forest, and cotton plantations had all been exhausted, the region, for all practical purposes, was abandoned. No politicians stepped forward to inject transfusions of government funds into the development of the infrastructure of this region. No plans were set forth for the economic development of this region. No plans were implemented for attracting new industry to this area. Politicians' self-serving agendas and indifference to the plight of this region contributed greatly to the continued decline in this isolated area.

From 1901 until 1961, the Alabama State Legislature was controlled and dominated by a few wealthy land owners and former plantation owners. These wealthy citizens, almost all being from the southern tier of Alabama counties, used gerrymandering skills to gain an unfair advantage in state government. While the vast number of citizens now lived in urban areas such as Birmingham, these wealthy land owners were successful in preventing the redistricting or redefining of the political boundaries of the state for over fifty years! Large sums of government funds were distributed for pet projects and lucrative political pots in these relatively sparsely settled southern counties while the more densely settled industrial northern counties were left to struggle just for survival. For decades, this small wealthy rural minority of Alabama citizens dominated the state government. The need for urban development and industrialization was not addressed. They were comfortable and content with conditions just the way they were. Approximately 50 percent of Alabama's citizens were disenfranchised and unable to vote until 1961. All blacks and many poor whites were not permitted to vote. Change usually comes very slowly in government, especially if there is a reluctance to promote change by those in power.

On a recent trip to this small town and ridge (2015), I observed the plight of this region appearing even more desperate than ever. Little, if anything, has been done to attract industry to this region. High school graduates in this area today face the same dilemma that others have faced year after year for more than a half century. Graduate, then ask the question, "Now what? I must leave this area. No jobs here, just like it was fifty years ago." So little change since the '30s, '40s, '50s, '60s, '70s, '80s, '90s, 2000s. So little change.

Overview

Hi, Tim,

Approximately ten months ago, I began writing you a few letters I thought you might be interested in, which described my childhood years from birth to eighteen years old. What began as letters evolved into somewhat of a novel based on the real life adventures and experiences of a young child growing up in a very unique time and in a very unique place. As I wrote, I had two objectives in mind; first I hoped to portray my first-hand experiences of what it was like growing up in this era and in this place. Secondly, I hoped to paint a picture of the rapidly changing and evolving American culture across the country during this same era. I began with my preschool years, then my elementary school years, my junior high school years, and finally, my high school days. By describing my family, father and mother, brothers and sisters, the small town, and the ridge people, as well as a brief history of the area, I hoped to present a background which would be helpful in understanding the unique nature of this time and place.

Obviously, my perspective changed during this eighteen-year-period with my maturation. My experiences, observations, and feelings as a preschool child in the mid-

1930s was probably not much different than had I been born five or ten years later in the '40s or '50s. Even though the depression era was very difficult for families and the nation as a whole, for a preschool age child, they were good years. I was too young to sense any of the economic turmoil and crisis facing our country. Having a sense of a secure home environment with stability and safety was basically all that was needed in those formidable years. My horizons were quite limited, not being much aware of anything beyond the home environment and the family farm. Being surrounded by nature, which I thoroughly enjoyed, I had practically all my needs met. The forest, fields, farm animals, brothers and sisters, and a mother and father assured my preschool years were filled with happiness, security, and contentment. Had I been born in the '40s or '50s and been exposed to the same environment and secure family ties, I feel confident my preschool years would have been equally enjoyable in those times as well.

My second objective was to enlighten you as to the profound changes which took place during this era and to understand the overall impact of these changes on the country as a whole, but more especially on the rural folks and their culture. Evolving from horse-and-buggy days to major modernization in every aspect of society took place in less than two decades! It's practically impossible to adequately describe the impact of the post-war era industrialization and development of new technology and inventions such as television, jet engines, super highways, etc. Yet numerous remote regions of the country, such as Walker County, continued to flounder and struggle as if industrialization and modernization had just passed them by. Some rural folks felt secure and content in their rural environment. Their past ways of doing things were good enough for Ma and Pa and are good enough for me.

Some resisted all the changes as undesirable and feared they would destroy their heritage. Why change if the status quo had been in place for three or four generations and seemed to work just fine? Others struggled to get a piece of the pie, but many lacked the basic fundamentals to compete. Most of the younger generation had little choice except to abandon the region and seek a better standard of living elsewhere.

As I aged and became more aware of my expanding horizons, I began to understand the pressure to become a productive family member and a responsible student in school. Learning the proper protocol for acceptable school behavior and conduct within our social circle was emphasized early and frequently. This redefined who I was and what was expected of me. Things had changed from all play to less play and more work. I began cultivating more relationships outside the home environment.

Relatives, neighborhood friends, and school friends required developing social skills and appropriate conduct to maintain my acceptance in my social group.

Junior high, age twelve to fifteen, were the most difficult. Trying to make sense of the hormonal changes in my body, the growth spurt, and physical changes were confusing and mysterious. Was I still a child or was I a man? Why did I feel a need for more independence? Was I ready for it? Why was my relationship with my parents changing? Why the aggression? Why did I stutter and stammer when I tried to talk with a pretty girl?

High school years saw less confusion and more clarity about the realities of life. Would I be prepared to go out into the real world? Why did I, at times, feel very insecure about my preparation to face adult life? Due to where I was in this rural area, few options were available. It was obvious a high school graduate would have to seek his career or job elsewhere. Being so isolated from the real world around us made it very difficult to face the challenges ahead. I must abandon all my pillars of security and support and strike out on my own. There was so much I didn't know about life, and so very much more I would need to learn in order to compete. Uncertainty made that first step very difficult. Deep down inside, however, I knew it was time to take that first big step.

As the natural resources were exhausted and coal mining declined in Walker County, the fate of the small town was typical of approximately a dozen other small coal mining towns in Walker County. This is why I chose not to identify this specific town by its name. It seemed appropriate to let it represent all the small coal mining towns who suffered the same fate during this era.

In my sequels, I've tried to take a look at the bigger picture out and beyond the small town. Even though some remained isolated on the mountain, the real world was exploding with world and political crisis after crisis. Enormous changes and industrialization would eventually impact everyone, even those still isolated in these rural areas. No one escaped the trauma generated by World War II. Ten young men on the ridge were inducted into the military. Some were fortunate enough to make it home in one piece, others suffered serious injuries, and others lost their lives.

In the '50s, industrialization exploded in many northern states. This acted as a magnet, attracting and luring most of the younger generation of working families to new homes in distance cities. No more living on small rural family farms. No more horses, large barns, and hard work on rural farms; the city is the place to be.

Changes and more changes ushered in new lifestyles. Television, space travel, advances in medicine, social unrest, computers, and of course, the sixty years of Cold War all had a huge impact on America.

The Elliott clan was not immune from all these changes. Only one of the seven now remains in the small town. When they retired, all the others chose to live elsewhere. During the '60s, a refreshing breeze of good fortune came to Vora and Jonny. They sold twenty acres of the original homestead and farm to a man who desired to build a home on this site which had a commanding view overlooking the small town. Also, through either a class action lawsuit against the coal mining industry or else through the Federal Department of Social Security, Jonny was awarded a lump sum pay-off settlement due to his black lung disease. This money received from these sources assured them a comfortable living during their older years.

Unfortunately, both Jonny and Vora were killed in a tragic automobile accident on December 9, 1979. Vora was seventy-six and Jonny was eighty-four at the time of their deaths. John Jr. retired from Auburn University and built a nice home in a wonderful grove of stately pecan trees in Auburn. He passed away January 27, 2011. He is survived by his wife, Hazel, and two sons, Joe and Greg.

James retired from the Department of Social Security and spent his retirement years in Birmingham. He died on June 13, 2008. His wife, Novis, died on May 22, 2010. James and Novis are survived by two children, Jim and Jeannie. They both have three children and Jim has one grandchild.

Frances survived the untimely death of her first husband, James Eason, who passed away on April 26, 1977. They had two children, Woody and Dennis. Woody and Dennis each have two children. Frances remarried Lawrence Williams from Florence, Alabama. Due to cancer, Frances died on June 8, 1996.

Vera retired as a teacher in the public schools in the Birmingham area. Her husband, Garland, was also a school principle. They retired to a home they built near Trussville, Alabama. Garland passed away on January 14, 2006, and Vera died on August 7, 2013. They are survived by their son, Ben, and his wife, Lydia. Ben has two children, Laura and Leslie, and one grandchild.

Fred retired from the Redstone Arsenal in Huntsville, Alabama. Upon retiring, he moved back to the small town and lives with his wife, Romaine. Fred is eighty-two years old. They have two children, Mark and Matt. Both Mark and Matt have two children.

Lois lost her first husband, Bobby Duncan, on December 3, 1999. She remarried Mack Lyon from Oklahoma. Lois and Mack are currently living in Edmund, Oklahoma. Lois and Bobby had two children, Jill and Tim. Jill has two children, a boy and a girl, and Tim has one son.

Louis lives with his wife, Carolyn, in the small resort town of Caseville, Michigan. They have three children, Don, Dale, and Lori. Don lives in Southern California, while Dale and Lori live in the Detroit suburbs. Louis and Carolyn have five grandchildren: Jason Elliott, Leanne Richardson, Tim Mason, Jenna Mason, and Kara Mason, and there are four great-grandchildren.

> Now abideth faith, hope, and love, these
> three, but the greatest of these is love.

Written in loving memory and honor of my parents and all my brothers and sisters.

The seventh child,
Louis

1895-1920 Pa Jim and his "Mail Delivering Buggy"

(1942) Front row- left, Louis, Lois, Fred
Back row- James, Jonny, Vora, Vera, Frances

John Jr. --Age ? (20-22)

James- age 17

(1942-45) James somewhere in France or Belgium

Frances–age 18

Vera–age 17

Most Intellectual
Most Likely to succeed - FRED ELLIOTT

Lois–age 17

Louis–age 17

(1942) Lois, Fred, Louis showing their patriotism
by wearing big brother's army hats

Louis–age 15

1941 John Jr. and his Ford coupe in California

LEE THORNBERRY   MISS ALABAMA 1958

Dear Uncle Louis,

I wanted to tell you how much Linda and I enjoyed the book about Elliott family life on the "ridge". Your remembrances helped me to better appreciate life there in the small town I already had good memories of the ridge myself and these stories have deepened my appreciation of the special farm where my mom grew up.

The book has given me a greater appreciation of my grandparents and what they went through to make the little farmhouse on the ridge into a home where everyone was loved. It is obvious that a sense of community was fostered which led everyone to contribute what they could to make life better. The character and success of my aunts and uncles attest to the Christian upbringing that happened there. We plan to share those stories with our own children and grandchildren so they will know more about their rich family heritage.

Thanks again,

Dennis
Dennis

About the Author

After leaving Walker County, Alabama, in December 1954, the author, Louis Elliott, made his way to the Detroit, Michigan area. He began working in various manufacturing factories which supplied parts for the automobile industry. In 1958, he earned his degree in industrial education from Wayne State University. He then took a job as a shop teacher in a local high school. He worked as a public school teacher for fifteen years before moving on to accept a position as the administrator over a health care campus consisting of a nursing home, independent senior housing complex, and an assisted living facility. He remained with this not-for-profit health care facility for twenty years before retiring in 2000. He moved to the Caseville, Michigan, area in 2004. He began working on his book in the fall of 2014 and completed it in midsummer of 2015. He and his wife, Carolyn, still live in the thumb area of Michigan.

CPSIA information can be obtained
at www.ICGtesting.com
Printed in the USA
FFHW01n0920010818
47601495-51116FF